Ever since **Lisa Childs** rea~~~~~~~~~~~~
at age eleven—a Mills & B~~~~~~~~~~~~
all she wanted was to be a romance writer. With
over forty novels~~~~~~~~

LISA CHILDS

Printed and bound in Spain
by CPI, Barcelona

MILLS & BOON

First Published in Great Britain 2018
by Mills & Boon, an imprint of HarperCollins*Publishers*
1 London Bridge Street, London, SE1 9GF

© 2018 Lisa Childs

ISBN: 978-0-263-93235-5

CHAPTER ONE

"I AM GOING to prove to you that this man is a bad man," the assistant district attorney said as she pointed at the defense table.

Stone Michaelsen had the uneasy feeling that she was pointing at him rather than his client. But it wasn't as if he could object. He was a bad man—sometimes.

And right now, watching Hillary Bellows work the jury, he wanted to be very bad to her. She was so damn sexy in her sky-blue suit that perfectly matched her sky-blue eyes. The skirt fit tightly over her rounded ass, and the jacket didn't quite close over her full breasts, showing off her flesh-colored camisole. She had the rapt attention of every male juror and, since she was so earnest, most of the women as well. When she turned back toward the jury, her blond bob skimmed across her jaw. Her hair looked so silky that his fingers twitched to touch it, to touch her.

But as always, when he faced her in court, he had to resist the urge to act on this crazy attraction he had for her. Hillary Bellows was strictly off-limits. But even if she wasn't, she had made it abundantly clear that she didn't think much of him. He would really have to turn on the charm if he wanted to change her mind about him.

And, unlike his law partners, Stone was not a natural charmer. He was too blunt and outspoken to be ingratiating and flattering. So was Hillary.

She continued her opening statement. "I am going to prove beyond a reasonable doubt that the defendant murdered his young wife in a jealous rage. The defendant's attorney, Stone Michaelsen, from the notorious Street Legal law practice, is going to try to trick you into exonerating his client—because he and his partners will do anything to win."

Stone resisted the urge to flinch—barely. She was hitting low, even for Hillary, using the recent problems his firm had been having against him. And the problems weren't their fault; they had a mole in the office, someone trying to throw their cases and make them look bad. If she'd had access to their case files, he might have thought Hillary was the one responsible for the leaks.

She seemed to be carrying a grudge against him from all the times he'd beaten her before—because her opening argument felt more like a personal attack against him than a summary of the case she was going to present.

"And like his partners," Hillary continued, "Stone Michaelsen will use the media and other tricks to make his case, because he has no evidence."

He suppressed a flinch at her direct hit. He had a meeting later with Allison McCann of McCann Public Relations. They were going to discuss his next press release. The publicist had already issued statements from his office about the prosecution disregarding the fact that his client had an ironclad alibi for the time of the murder. Charges never should have been brought against Byron Mueller. And the grand jury should have damn well never indicted. But because of that alibi, this would be an easy win for Stone, and another loss for Hillary.

Maybe that was why she sounded so bitter in this opening statement. She knew she was going to lose, just as she had every other time she had gone up against him in court. What if she were literally up against him? All her lush curves pressed against his body?

Now he had to suppress a smile. He couldn't have the jury thinking he looked smug, even though he felt smug at the moment.

But Hillary looked pretty damn smug herself. She glanced at him again—instead of his client—and there was a glimmer of amusement in her blue eyes. What the hell did she find so funny?

It wouldn't be the fact that she was going to lose. She wouldn't find that funny at all, not with as ambitious as she was.

Then she turned away from him and focused on the jury again. She lowered her voice, as if confiding a big secret to them, and said, "Even the alibi his client claims to have for the time of the murder has been discredited with evidence from Mr. Michaelsen's own case files."

What the hell was she talking about? Stone jumped out of his chair and protested, "Your Honor, I object. The assistant DA is making an inculpatory statement—"

"That I can prove," Hillary interrupted him.

The gavel slammed down. "This is Ms. Bellows's opening argument, Mr. Michaelsen. You will have the chance to defend your client during the trial."

"Sounds like I'm the one who needs defending," he grumbled as he reluctantly settled back into his seat.

"Mr. Michaelsen…" the judge said, his voice sharp with a warning. Harrison had ruled the bench for a long time, probably too long. What wispy hair he had left was white, and his face was heavily lined with age and disapproval.

It was never good for Stone when he drew Harrison as a judge. But still, he had to appeal to the guy.

"Please remind Ms. Bellows that my law firm is not on trial here," he said. "Only my client."

The judge didn't give Hillary a verbal warning, just a pointed glare that Hillary then passed on to Stone, her blue eyes narrowing. But a slight smile curved her lips. She was obviously enjoying needling him.

He found his pulse racing as well, and not just over the thrill of a high-profile trial, but over the thrill of facing her again. He'd beaten her before, but it hadn't been easy. As a lawyer, she'd proved to be his greatest challenge.

As a woman...

No. Because she was a lawyer, specifically his opposing counsel on this case, he couldn't think of her as a woman. But that was damn hard.

He wouldn't mind Hillary going below his belt, as long as she was not hitting him. Hell, he'd really love her going below his belt and zipper and boxers.

Stone's client nudged his arm. "This isn't looking good," he murmured with genuine concern. "What's she talking about, your case files discrediting my alibi?"

"I don't know," Stone whispered back. But he was damn well going to find out.

"Mr. Michaelsen, Ms. Bellows has the floor. You and your client need to save your discussion for after court."

Stone flinched. Great. He'd already pissed off the judge. Of course, Judge Harrison usually seemed pissed off, even before the trial started.

Stone squeezed his client's arm, trying to reassure him, but Byron Mueller suddenly looked every one of his sixty-some years. The billionaire was known for being all brash, bluster and bravado, but then, he hadn't ever gotten into any trouble before that he hadn't been able to buy his way out of. By hiring Stone and Street Legal, he must have thought he would buy his way out of this, too. But the murder charge was serious.

And so was Hillary Bellows, as she continued her opening statement about all the reasons why the jury should find his client guilty. Of course, her biggest reason seemed to be Stone—like Byron Mueller wouldn't have hired him if he wasn't guilty.

The problem was: he wasn't. No matter what Hillary thought she had learned from Stone's case files—that alibi was real. Byron was innocent, and Stone intended to prove it. But if Hillary managed to throw out the alibi, that was going to be damn hard… almost as hard as Stone got just watching the beautiful assistant district attorney work.

Hillary Bellows didn't care how late it was. She was not at all tired, not with all the excitement coursing through her. She couldn't stop smiling. She was going to win this time. Stone Michaelsen was not going to get his client off—like he had so many others.

She leaned back in her desk chair and thought

of the stunned expression on his ridiculously handsome face during her opening argument. She'd taken him by surprise, which unsettled her a bit. How had she gotten that information if it hadn't come from his office?

It didn't matter, though.

She was going to win. Of course, she wouldn't be able to celebrate the way she'd have liked—with Stone getting *her* off. He was so damn good-looking with his thick black hair and those deep gray eyes of his. And his body...

With his broad shoulders, big chest and arms, and heavy thighs, his body was as ridiculously perfect as his handsome face.

How could he be in such good shape? He was always trying a case, so he had to work almost as hard as she did. And she never found time to get to the gym. So how did he?

He had to lift weights a lot. A lot of weights...

Or maybe he lifted a lot of women. She wanted him to lift her—to carry her effortlessly in those big strong arms of his. To carry her off to his bedroom...

She snorted at her fantasy. That was all it was ever going to be: just a fantasy. Unfortunately, she had a lot of them about Stone Michaelsen.

She uttered a wistful sigh and reached for the candy bar that was her dinner. Or maybe dessert now, since the dinner hour had passed a while ago. She closed her eyes as the smooth dark chocolate dissolved on her tongue, teasing her taste buds with the paradox of sweet and bitterness. A little moan of pleasure slipped through her lips.

A groan echoed it.

Startled, she jumped and nearly fell out of her chair as she opened her eyes to find Stone Michaelsen leaning against the doorjamb of her office. She hadn't left that open; she never did, but especially not after hours. But then, maybe the cleaning crew had when one of them had taken her trash earlier. She'd said they could come back and finish cleaning a little later, but she suspected they'd already left for the night since that had been a while ago.

"How the hell did you get in here?" she asked.

How had she not heard the door open? How had she not felt him watching her? Had she been that preoccupied…thinking about him?

He lifted one of his broad shoulders in a half shrug. "I'm not such a bad man that I can't make it past security," he said with a grin, "especially when I represented the guard's grandson for a drug charge."

She glared at him. "Of course you did." And she suspected that he'd either gotten the charges reduced or tossed out.

He had no chance of getting the charges in his current case tossed out. Or reduced.

But she had no doubt that was why he was here.

She leaned back in her chair and studied him. "So, let me guess… You want to talk plea deal?"

"I have a plea for you," he said as he stepped inside her office and closed the door.

The room was already small, but now it seemed to shrink even more as he filled it. He was so damn big—over six feet of height and breadth. His thick black hair looked a little mussed now, as if he'd run his hands through it. Or maybe some woman just had. And his gray eyes, they were so intense and focused…on her.

Her pulse quickened as he approached her desk. He braced his palms on top of the files on it and leaned over, so that his face was nearly level with hers. Now her pulse raced. Was his plea for a kiss?

She was tempted to close the distance between them and press her lips to his. But she knew that wasn't what he wanted. He wouldn't—couldn't—want *her*.

He and his law partners dated lingerie models, fashion designers, actresses and heiresses—not poorly paid, overworked assistant district attorneys like she was. But this was the career and the life she had chosen. And she was good with that, and even better that she could have him only in her fantasies. That was a hell of a lot safer than the reality of Stone Michaelsen.

Because she did not want the real Stone Michaelsen. He was arrogant, ruthless and amoral. No. She just wanted the fantasy one who didn't speak, who only kissed and caressed her.

"Don't you want to know my plea?" he asked.

She drew in a deep breath to bring herself to her senses. But she only breathed in his scent, which was soap, musk and something that was him alone. "For mercy?" she teased. "You have never showed me any."

Not in court. And not in those damn press releases he had that PR firm issue for him. Curiously, there had not been one printed today. And she would have thought it would have been more important today—than any other day—for him to discredit her case.

But then, he knew he couldn't discredit the evidence that had been sent from his own office. Why had he done that, though? It wasn't like Stone Michaelsen to play by the rules, or even to play fair.

"You're not my client," he told her. "I only plead for my clients."

He usually didn't plea them out, though. He came up with some ridiculous defense instead. And no matter how ridiculous it was, he conned the jury into buying it.

What the hell was he going to come up with this time? She could hardly wait to find out.

She shook her head. "I'm not giving your client any mercy. No plea deals for him." Stone had wasted his time coming to see her.

"I wouldn't accept a plea deal for him," Stone said. "Byron Mueller is innocent."

She snorted. Who was living in a fantasy world now? "If you repeat the lie enough times, do you start to believe it?"

His gray eyes narrowed in a glare. Obviously, he didn't like being called a liar. But it was what he was, what he did. And Hillary always called it like she saw it.

"No. Really. I'm curious," she continued. "I don't understand how defense lawyers do it." How could they represent someone they knew was guilty?

But that apparently was not what Stone thought she was talking about, because now his gray eyes glittered with amusement. Wriggling his brows suggestively, he lowered his voice to a sexy whisper and murmured, "I could show you."

Her heart stopped beating entirely for a moment. Was he flirting with her?

Stone Michaelsen didn't flirt. He was too focused on winning trials—on always being the best. Was he that way in the bedroom, too?

Did he have to be the best?

It wasn't as if she would ever find out, though. He wasn't suggesting what she'd thought he was. No. She must have been fantasizing yet. He wasn't even here, let alone uttering innuendos. She reached under her desk and pinched the top of her thigh. Then she tried not to flinch at the pain.

She wasn't fantasizing. This was real. Stone Michaelsen was in her office, and he was…

Flirting.

With.

Her.

CHAPTER TWO

WHAT THE HELL was he doing?

Stone hadn't come to the district attorney's office to flirt with Hillary Bellows. He'd come to get answers from her, to find out what the hell she'd been talking about in court about documents from his office. But now he just wanted to make her come.

And he really, really wanted to come himself.

Being alone with her had been a very bad idea. But he'd been so angry about her opening argument that he hadn't thought his attraction to her would be an issue. Then he'd found her leaning back in her desk chair, moaning...

And all he could think about was making her moan again—with his kiss, with his touch...

Her face flushed a bright pink as she stared at him, her blue eyes widened with shock, the same shock he felt that he'd said what he had. Then she stammered, "I—I don't want to know how defense lawyers do it."

"Why not?" Stone asked. "Because you find us all beneath you?"

Then he groaned at the image that flashed into his mind—of being beneath her as she rode him in a frenzy, trying to reach the release from the tension that had already begun to build inside him.

As if this damn trial wasn't making him tense enough.

Now he'd lost his grip on this attraction he felt for her. That he had always felt for her.

Did she feel nothing in return?

She shivered and murmured, "I don't know how you do it."

"And I offered to show you," he said, and he was just as surprised as he'd been the first time the innuendo had slipped out. Was he flirting?

The guys would have laughed if they'd heard him. They always razzed him about being incapable of smooth-talking; they claimed that he just went up to women and grunted at them.

"Mr. Michaelsen!" she exclaimed.

And he chuckled. "Look at you, Ms. Bellows. All outraged self-righteousness. I understand now why you work hard. You obviously have your sights set on the bench someday."

"What?" she asked, her brow puckering with confusion.

"You want to be a judge," he said. "You're certainly all judgy right now." Which should have turned him off. But he could picture her wearing only one of those black robes with nothing beneath it…

But his hands.

He was losing his fucking mind. And it was all her fault. She'd unsettled him even more today than she usually did, and it wasn't just because of her beauty.

Damn, she was beautiful, though. So beautiful.

Her eyes were so clear and blue and full of intelligence with thick black lashes fringing them. Her face was round with wide cheekbones and a pointed little chin that he saw so often tilted with pride and the self-righteousness of which he'd accused her. And her lips, which were usually pulled into a pucker of disapproval, were full and red and temptingly kissable. Especially now…with chocolate smeared at the corner of her mouth.

He wanted to kiss it away. He wanted to kiss her—so badly that his stomach muscles were tightened and his cock was hard and pulsating with desire.

But before he could close the distance between his mouth and hers, she jumped up from her chair—as if she knew what he'd intended. "I want justice," she said, "for poor Bethany Mueller and all the other victims of your clients."

He could understand that, but in this case, Byron was truly innocent. And Stone had thought he'd had the alibi to prove it. "If you actually want justice for Bethany, you should drop these charges against Byron. He didn't kill his wife."

She snorted. "I knew that's why you came here," she said. "Just to get the charges tossed out or reduced." Despite her assertion, disappointment flickered through her eyes.

Had she wanted him here for another reason? Did she want him like he wanted her?

His body tensed even more than it had been, his cock throbbing behind his fly. Good thing he was still wearing his suit jacket, or she might have seen how much she affected him. And he had no doubt she would use that attraction against him in court.

Unless she felt it, too.

A thrill raced through him. But he didn't know if it was excitement or fear. If she was attracted to him, too, he had no hope of resisting her.

It had been hard enough to fight it when he'd thought the attraction was just one-sided. But now...

He shook his head, but he couldn't shake off the desire he felt for her. "I'm not here to get the charges thrown out or reduced," he said, repeating what he'd already told her. Although, it would have made his case a hell of a lot easier if she would just take his word for Byron Mueller's innocence.

"Then why are you here?" she asked. "You said you had a plea for me."

He'd had one when he'd walked in. Now all he

could think about was kissing that chocolate off her mouth. She was so damn sexy.

"What's your plea?" she prodded him.

And he wanted to plea for that kiss…

Was he staring at her mouth? Hillary couldn't be certain but it felt as if his gaze was focused there, on her lips. Did he want to kiss her as badly as she wanted him to? If she hadn't stood up when she had, she might have leaned forward and brushed her mouth across his.

She'd been so damn tempted.

Earlier she'd been cold in her office. Now heat rushed through her—so much heat that it burned in her core—for him. Afraid she might start sweating if she didn't get cooler, she stripped off her jacket and tossed it over the back of her chair.

His eyes turned dark, the pupils swallowing the silvery gray, and a muscle twitched in his cheek just above his rigidly clenched jaw. A shadow of a beard already darkened his skin, even though he'd been cleanly shaven in court that morning. He looked tense and edgy, like he was barely holding on to his control.

Her heart beat faster and erratically.

He looked as if he might dive across her desk and grab her and take her. At least in her mind, that was how he looked. But that was probably just because of all the fantasies she'd had about him.

Why did he have to be so damn good-looking?

It wasn't fair that the opposing counsel was so ir-resistibly sexy.

Hillary was all about fairness. That was why she'd become a lawyer. She doubted Stone had had the same altruistic reasons for going to law school and passing the bar. She guessed that money, more than justice, had motivated him and his partners to become lawyers. Street Legal was the highest-priced law firm in New York City.

And that was saying something.

That was why only billionaires like Byron Mueller could afford to have Stone Michaelsen represent them. The guard's grandson must have had a richer relative who had paid Stone's fee to get that drug charge reduced. Because Stone didn't care about justice. She wasn't even sure how much he really cared about the money. She suspected he cared most about winning. And that he would do whatever necessary to triumph.

So she didn't doubt that he might try to seduce her to get the upper hand for his client. Maybe he thought she'd go easy on Mueller if he romanced her. That possibility sobered her up; she was no longer drunk on desire for him. Since he'd never flirted with her before, it was more a probability than a possibility that he was up to something.

Her heart rate slowed and weariness weighed on her, reminding her that it had been one damn long day.

"What do you want, Stone?" she asked him and then yawned. "It's late, and I need to get home."

"Someone waiting for you?" he asked.

Did he sound jealous? Of her?

Now she was losing it entirely. He wasn't really interested in her; he was just playing her to get his client off. He wasn't going to get her off...like she wanted, like she needed.

Maybe she should call someone to meet her at her apartment. Dwight? Since meeting in law school, they'd been casually seeing each other: getting together for drinks to discuss cases and blow off steam. But wasn't he seriously seeing someone now?

No. She couldn't call him. A public defender had asked for her number a couple of weeks ago, but she hadn't given it to him. He'd given her his, though, hadn't he? If she could find his number, maybe she could call him. But she couldn't remember what he looked like now.

She couldn't think of anyone but Stone Michaelsen. That was just because he was there—filling her small office with his presence and his scent and his sexy-as-sin body.

"That's a long pause," he said. "I can't believe you don't have anyone waiting for you. Husband? Fiancé? Boyfriend?"

"I didn't say I don't have anyone waiting," she pointed out.

"No," he agreed. "You didn't say anything at all."

And he trailed off, as if waiting for her to say something.

Her lips curved into a slight smile at his persistence. "That's a personal question," she said. "And we don't do personal, Stone."

She might have gotten a drink with another lawyer or had lunch with him. But not Stone. She'd refused every time he'd asked her out after a case.

She'd suspected then that he'd only wanted to gloat about his victory. And she'd been too furious over the loss...of justice.

His eyes flared again, going dark and sparkly with desire. Or was she only imagining that. "I love the way you say my name," he murmured, his voice gruff.

She shivered now. Of course, she was wearing only a thin camisole since she'd taken off her jacket. His gaze moved down, to where her nipples were pressing through her lace bra and pushing against the silk of her camisole.

"Sto—Mr. Michaelsen," she said, putting the same warning in her tone that Judge Harrison had used with him that afternoon.

He grinned. "Oh, Hillary... I think we could have some fun being personal."

Now the heat flashed back through her, heating her face and her entire body. Her patience, as well as her control, wearing thin, she asked, "Why are you here?"

He didn't reply. He just kept staring at her with that glint of naughtiness in his eyes.

"If you're not going to tell me," she said, "I'm going to leave."

But that would mean walking around him to get to the door, and she didn't want to get any closer to him. Not right now…

Not with the way he was looking at her.

He closed his eyes, breaking that connection between them. When he opened them again, he shook his head and rubbed one hand around the nape of his neck, as if he was stressed.

After her opening argument, he should be stressed.

She had him this time. And he had to know it as well as she did.

"I came here to find out what the hell you were talking about in your opening statement when you claimed to have evidence from my case files," he said.

She relaxed and smiled. "It's the truth. I have evidence—"

"I want to know how the hell you got anything from my case files!" he said, his voice rising with irritation.

He obviously had no idea. A laugh slipped through her lips. Yes, she had him. He was not winning this time.

"You're talking about the evidence that proves your client's alibi is fake," she said.

He shook his head again, but this time vehemently. "It's not fake."

"The bank records you sent me prove that Mr. Mueller bought and paid for that alibi," she reminded him. How could Stone have not realized that? But then, it didn't sound as if he'd actually meant to share those records with her.

Which he confirmed when he said, through gritted teeth, "I did not send you anything."

"Someone from your office did," she said. And she still could not believe her good fortune. She hadn't expected to get *any* help from the defense for the prosecution, let alone this much.

Now he chuckled. "I wouldn't be so cocky, Hillary. You got played by our office mole."

"What?" She narrowed her eyes and studied him with suspicion. What game was he playing with her now? "What the hell are you talking about? What would an office mole have to do with me?"

The humor left his face as his jaw went rigid with anger. "We have a little issue. Someone has been trying to cause problems for the practice. Until now, only my partners have been affected."

She could believe that Street Legal had made some enemies—because for every case they won, someone else lost. But she wasn't really buying his story. It sounded too much like one of the press releases that PR firm put out for them for damage control.

Why hadn't he issued one today?

"The last time someone received something supposedly from our case files," he continued, "the documents had been forged." The grin curved his lips up again. "So I wouldn't be so confident about your evidence."

She narrowed her eyes and studied his handsome face. "You're bluffing," she said. And she hoped like hell that he was.

He had to be or he would have had McCann issue a statement that the evidence was forged. If he could prove that it was... He was the one with no proof.

His grin only widened. "You'll see that I'm telling the truth when my client is acquitted."

She hated his smugness. She hated a lot of things about Stone Michaelsen. That was why she would only ever fantasize about him and would never actually act on her attraction to him. But because they were alone and she was more aware of him than she'd ever been, she needed to get away from him before she forgot how much she hated about him.

She snagged her jacket from the back of her chair and grabbed her briefcase from the desk. "I'm leaving," she said. "We have an early morning in court." She probably shouldn't have reminded him of that. Let him be late. Judge Harrison would love that.

"So nobody's waiting for you at home," he said.

She sighed and shook her head as she moved to step around him. But before she could maneuver past him, he wrapped his arms around her and jerked her up against his long, hard body. Then he lowered his mouth to hers.

First, his lips just brushed across hers. Then his tongue flicked out and licked the corner of her mouth. "Sweet…" he said.

And heat flushed her face as she realized she'd had chocolate on her face the entire time they'd been talking. But they weren't talking now. He moved his mouth over hers again, and she gasped for breath as panic and attraction squeezed her lungs.

He deepened the kiss, sliding his tongue inside her mouth. She tasted the chocolate. Dark and rich, and just a touch bitter. Then she tasted him. And he tasted the same.

There was nothing really sweet about the chocolate or his flavor. But it was intoxicating.

And addictive…

She trembled with the force of the desire rushing through her, and the jacket and briefcase handle slipped through her shaking hands. When they were free, she reached for him. Sliding her fingers into his thick black hair, she held his head down as she kissed him back.

CHAPTER THREE

WHAT THE HELL had he done? Kissing Hillary Bellows had been a huge mistake. But it was a mistake that Stone wanted to repeat over and over again.

Fingers snapped in front of his face. "What the hell's wrong with you, Stone?" Ronan Hall grumbled at him. "You called this damn emergency meeting, and you haven't said a word yet."

He shook his head and murmured, "Sorry."

"Allison McCann said you stood her up for your meeting yesterday afternoon, too," Simon Kramer remarked from the head of the conference table in his office. He was the managing partner of Street Legal, just as the young con artist had been the managing partner when they'd all been living on the streets as teen runaways.

"I called her and canceled," Stone said. At least he thought he had. He hadn't talked to Allison directly but he'd left a message with her assistant.

He'd wanted to talk to Hillary before he issued

any more press releases. If only all he had done was talk…

But being alone with her, and in such a small space, had tested his control in a way it had never been tested with her before. Hell, he didn't think his control in general had ever been tested like that before. It was probably the first test he'd ever failed in his life.

"You look like hell," Simon remarked.

"He's got a tough trial," Trevor Sinclair said in his defense. Trev handled the biggest cases in their firm—all the class-action stuff that made them millions. "He probably didn't get any sleep."

Stone hadn't, and he wished that had been because of the trial. But that had all been because of the opposing counsel—his gorgeous, hot, passionate opposing counsel.

"I've never known Stone to lose much sleep over a trial," Simon said, and his blue eyes narrowed as he studied Stone's face.

He was careful to veil his expression, but Simon was good at reading people. As a con artist, he'd had to be in order to pick his marks. He hadn't been a con artist for a long time, but he hadn't lost any of his skills.

His skill was part of what had made Street Legal so successful. Their office encompassed the entire floor of a building in Midtown. It had hardwood floors, exposed brick and tall windows that looked out over the city.

Stone squinted at the sunshine streaming through the blinds of Simon's windows. "It wasn't the trial that cost me sleep," he admitted.

But he didn't own up to what had happened with Hillary Bellows. For one, his partners probably wouldn't believe it. Hell, he wasn't sure he believed it. Instead, he shared the news for which he'd called the early morning meeting. "That damn mole has struck again."

His partners all cursed. Simon cursed the loudest; he was especially frustrated that he hadn't caught the damn culprit yet. As managing partner, he'd assumed the responsibility for the leak and for stopping it.

"We need to put an end to this bullshit," Simon said, his voice nearly hoarse with anger. "Now."

Stone heartily agreed, and he regretted not getting involved in the search sooner. But he'd been preparing his case for trial. And…

Until now, he hadn't been affected.

The mole had struck Trevor first with a leak of case files to opposing counsel. But Trevor had won the big class-action lawsuit despite it.

Stone wasn't convinced he could handle the mole's attack as well as Trevor had. Hell, he already hadn't.

"What happened?" Ronan asked. He'd been the latest victim before Stone.

"Hillary Bellows received something from our

office," he explained. "Something she thought was in my case files. And it's big." He expelled a ragged breath. "It's something that could destroy my entire defense if it's true." Because his entire defense was hinged on that alibi. Without it…

"You don't know if it's true?" Ronan asked. At least the stuff that had been leaked about him had been forged. And neither he nor any of his partners had had any doubts about that.

Unfortunately, Stone had begun to have a few doubts—not about Ronan, but about his case. Maybe it was because he knew Hillary was good—so good that she wouldn't have brought up the evidence, even in her opening argument, if she hadn't confirmed its validity first. She wouldn't have been that careless and she certainly wouldn't have been that trusting, especially of anything she'd thought he'd sent her.

She didn't trust him at all. So why had she…?

Stone said, "I hope like hell that it isn't true."

And he wasn't talking about just the evidence but about last night. What the hell had he been thinking to kiss the attorney prosecuting his client?

But that wasn't the worst part of the night before. The worst part had been when she'd kissed him back.

Because then he'd lost all control.

How the hell had Hillary lost control like that? Her face was hot just thinking about the night before. She lifted one hand to her cheek and slapped it lightly. *Snap out of it.*

She had already spent too much time thinking about it. Too much time thinking about Stone Michaelsen, even before last night.

"Is that your pre-court ritual?" a male voice asked.

She whirled around to find her boss standing behind her in the hallway outside her office. He startled her so much that she nearly dropped the key she held near the lock.

She must have looked stunned because he added an explanation. "Slapping yourself in the face? Is that the way you get fired up?"

"Uh…" She couldn't think at all right now.

He chuckled. "Or maybe you use it to wake up."

She didn't need to wake up since she hadn't even slept. "I'm awake," she assured her boss.

The guy was short, nearly as short as she was, and he had the little man–Napoleon complex thing going on where he had to be in control at all times. More a dictator than a leader.

"Good," he said. "You need to be wide awake to take on Stone Michaelsen." He cursed. "To take on any of those slick bastards from Street Legal."

He'd taken on Stone before and had lost just as she had. But his biggest loss was when Ronan Hall had represented his ex-wife in his recent divorce. Hillary kind of thought he'd deserved to lose that one, though. He was a bit of a lech.

Even the way he was looking at her now made her want to button up her jacket to her neck. But the button across her breasts was already straining. She needed to lay off the candy bars for dinner. Salads from now on.

From the way he was watching her, Wilson Tremont didn't seem to mind that she was carrying a few extra pounds, though. He had to be nearly twenty years older than her thirty years. Maybe he had even more years than that on her.

It was hard to tell with how he dyed his hair black and sprayed on a tan. He could have even been forty years older than she was.

"We need to win this case," he reiterated.

We? He wasn't sitting in on it with her—probably because he didn't want another loss on his record, especially with an election coming up. But she wasn't going to lose.

"And that damn alibi," he continued, "is going to make it tough for you. It was hard to even get the grand jury to indict with that." He had been surprised, and maybe also disappointed, that they had. He'd probably lost a potential supporter for his upcoming campaign.

But Hillary had had the murder weapon, which belonged to the defendant, and CSI had found only his prints on it. Hell, he'd had it locked up in a case to which he was the only one with a key. And the house staff and friends of Bethany's who'd testi-

fied that she had a lover had provided Byron's motive for killing his young bride. So Hillary had had
enough for the indictment. And now she had more
than enough to win.

But she didn't want to say that to her boss, or
Wilson Tremont would take the case from her and
try it himself. A win against Stone Michaelsen
would look good for him.

But Hillary wanted that win for herself.

Despite last night...

No. She couldn't think about last night right now.
Or at all.

"What are you doing here?" Wilson asked as he
glanced down at his watch. "Aren't you due in court
soon?"

She nodded, and her mouth went dry at the thought
of facing Stone so soon again. But she was a professional. She could do it—if only they had kept everything professional between them the night before.

But that was all his fault. He'd kissed her first.

...and she'd kissed him back.

But she hadn't been able to help herself. He'd tasted
so damn good, better than any candy bar she'd ever
eaten.

"I—I needed to get something that I left here last
night," she said.

Wilson nodded. "Notes."

"Yes." But she hesitated before unlocking the door.
She didn't want to open it with him standing there.

She wasn't sure exactly how she'd left it. Or where she'd left *it*.

"You better hurry up and get them, then," Wilson said with another glance at his watch. "You don't want to be late and piss off Judge Harrison."

No. She didn't. But she didn't want to risk anyone finding what she'd left in her office, either. Thankfully, the cleaning crew had left before she had last night. So she didn't think anyone had been inside since...

"I'll hurry," she promised as she slid the key into the lock. Just as she began to slowly turn the knob, someone called out for Wilson.

"Mr. Tremont, you have a call," his secretary told him. "The mayor..."

Wilson drew in a deep breath. "I hope he isn't calling about Mueller's case."

"Why would he?" Hillary asked, her brow furrowing with confusion.

Wilson smiled, but it was a patronizing one. "I forget how naive you can be, Hillary. You don't understand how politics work."

And he was probably damn happy about that, because he didn't think he had to worry about Hillary going after his job, like half the rest of the assistant district attorneys appeared to be doing. Hillary knew a lot more about politics than she was willing to admit. It was safer for her, though, if her boss didn't know that.

"I'm sure Mueller contributed to the mayor's campaign," Wilson explained. "Hell, I'll be lucky if the president doesn't call to give me heat over daring to prosecute the great Byron Mueller."

Hillary reached out and squeezed his arm, but she regretted her impulsive gesture when he glanced down at her hand on his coat sleeve. But even as she pulled back, she assured him, "Don't worry. Michaelsen is not going to get him off."

He stared at her, his dark eyes narrowed. "You're awfully confident, Hillary. I'd like to know why."

She gestured at his secretary. "You surely don't want to keep the mayor waiting, though." She didn't have to know how politics worked to know that that wouldn't be prudent. "And I don't want to be late for court."

Despite last night, she could face Stone again, because she knew she could and would beat him this time. Just as she could taste him yet on her lips, she could taste the sweetness of the victory that was sure to come.

"I can't piss off Judge Harrison," she reminded her boss.

He nodded. "Get moving, then."

He moved off down the hall toward his office and his on-hold call from the mayor, so Hillary pushed open her office door. And she was glad she'd waited until her boss had left before she'd opened it.

Stone's scent hung yet in the air—mixed with her

own. Just smelling that brought memories and sensations rushing back, and she experienced the heat and excitement of that passion all over again.

The kiss…

The…

And she lifted her hand to her cheek again. This time the slap wasn't quite as gentle. She needed to snap out of it. She had to face him—just minutes away—in the courtroom. And she had to pretend like nothing had happened.

But first she had to make sure that she'd left nothing behind to prove that it had. The space was small, so it was easy and quick to search.

But she couldn't find it.

What the hell had happened to it?

An alarm pealed out from the phone in her purse; it was her last-minute warning to get to the courtroom. She had no more time to search. Maybe the cleaning crew hadn't already been gone last night like she'd thought. Maybe they had cleaned her office after she'd left.

She closed and locked the door again before rushing off down the hall. She was still rushing when she walked into the courtroom, so she didn't even spare Stone a glance as she took her seat behind the prosecutor's table. She wouldn't have looked across the space between their tables at all if she hadn't felt him staring at her.

She didn't want to look at him. She dreaded to see

his amusement or his smugness over what had happened between them. Over what never should have happened between them.

When he'd kissed her, she should have slapped him—instead of kissing him back. But she'd been so shocked that she'd been beyond thought. At least beyond rational thought.

All she'd had in her head were those sick fantasies she had about him, about him kissing her just like he was.

So she'd kissed him back.

If only she had stopped at that.

Her face flushed from the heat of his gaze and from her embarrassment. Sure, she'd made a mistake. But she wasn't going to let that—or him—affect her. Just as she used to fantasize that something would happen between them, she was going to fantasize now that it hadn't.

She could only hope that he would do the same damn thing. But from the way she felt him looking at her, like he was touching her just as he had the night before, she knew that he wouldn't.

Despite her efforts to resist, his gaze drew hers. But when she glanced at him, he glanced down into his open briefcase. As she followed his gaze with hers, a gasp of shock slipped through her lips. Now she knew why she hadn't been able to find what she'd been looking for in her office.

She hadn't lost it there.

Stone had taken it.

A nude lace bra peeked out from beneath a manila folder in his briefcase.

"Son of a bitch," she whispered.

That was what he was. He'd used her—just as she'd worried he was using her. He'd gotten her off last night in the hopes of getting off his client.

Did he think she would forget all about the evidence that destroyed Byron Mueller's alibi?

He thought wrong. His little seduction had not changed her mind about him at all. In fact, it had proved what she'd already thought about him: Stone Michaelsen was a bad man.

But he didn't scare her.

Hillary was going to take him down and take him down hard—just like he'd taken her the night before.

CHAPTER FOUR

WHEN STONE HAD flashed Hillary a peek of what he'd hidden in his briefcase, she'd looked so surprised. But why? She'd said in her opening argument that he was a bad man. And after last night, she could have no doubt about just how bad Stone could be. He'd even surprised himself.

But when she'd kissed him back, something had happened to Stone that had never happened before. As she'd run her fingers up the nape of his neck and tunneled them through his hair, clasping his head to hers, her lips had moved so hungrily over his. She'd kissed him deeply—with her lips, with her tongue. And passion had overwhelmed him. He'd felt such a jolt of sexual awareness and energy. But he hadn't been the only one feeling it.

Because she'd moved her hands from his hair to the buttons of his shirt. She hadn't just undone them; she'd torn them open. Then she ran her hands over his chest, making his heart beat so fast and hard that he'd thought it would bust right out of him like his cock had tried busting right out of his fly.

"Hillary…" Her name had escaped his lips on a groan. She'd been torturing him with her touch, with her kiss.

And she'd broken his will to resist.

Not that he'd wanted to resist. He hadn't even intended to kiss her, though, when he'd come to her office. He'd only wanted to talk, to find out what the hell the evidence was that she'd bragged about having in court. But then he'd wanted to taste that chocolate on her mouth. He still hadn't intended to do anything other than kiss her then, though.

Until she'd kissed him back.

Then he'd reached for her clothes, like she'd reached for his. He pulled that camisole up and over her head. Beneath it she'd worn the lace bra that was now in his briefcase. Nude, so it wouldn't show through her clothes, it was practical and conservative, but the lace had made it sexy. And her breasts nearly spilling over the cups of the bra had made it even sexier. Like her…

She was sexy as hell.

Impossibly attracted to her, he'd unclasped her bra and feasted on her breasts. They were so full, the skin so silky, the nipples so taut and tempting. He nipped at one with his teeth, and she cried out his name.

Needing to know if he'd made her come, he slid his hand under her skirt, and he found her hot and wet and ready for him. So he lifted her onto her desk, knocking aside some folders that had already looked ready to topple. She hadn't uttered a protest at the mess he was making or over him touching her. Instead, she fumbled with his zipper and freed his erection. Her fingers slid around his cock and then up and down the length of it.

And he'd nearly come, too.

But he wanted more than a quick hand job. He wanted her. So he'd pulled back. And he fumbled a condom out of his wallet. Before he could tear it open, she'd taken it from his hand and torn it with her teeth.

And he'd groaned again, his cock throbbing with the tension gripping him. It had been so intense that it was almost painful. He'd needed a release more than he could ever remember needing one before.

He wanted her so badly that he nearly came when she rolled the condom over him. "Hillary…" He'd growled her name between gritted teeth.

And she'd giggled.

Stone didn't like to be laughed at, so he'd punished her. Instead of plunging inside her, he dropped to his knees. After pushing up her skirt, he tore her panties off. Then he teased her with his tongue, lapping at her until she arched off her desk and screamed his name.

She tasted sweeter than the chocolate he'd kissed off her mouth. So damn sweet. And she was so wet and hot for him that he'd thrust inside her then. Over and over again, he thrusted as she locked her legs around his waist. They'd moved together in a frenzy, desperate for release.

Her inner muscles had convulsed and clutched him as she came again. Then Stone's body had tensed and he'd shouted her name as he came—longer and more powerfully than he could remember having come in a long time.

Maybe it was just that it had been a long time since he'd been with someone. He'd been so busy getting ready for this case.

"Mr. Michaelsen!" Judge Harrison shouted his name. "Did you come to court this morning just to disrespect me?"

Stone blinked away the memories of the night before and glanced uneasily around. Everyone else in the courtroom was standing, including the judge. Stone was the only one sitting yet—in front of his briefcase with the bra sticking out from beneath a folder.

He jumped to his feet, hoping like hell that his suit coat hid the erection straining against his fly.

"I'm sorry, Your Honor," he said. He'd brought the bra to court to rattle Hillary. But it had had the reverse effect.

Last night she'd been the one rattled, so rattled that she'd pulled on her camisole and jacket and forgotten her bra as she'd struggled to collect all the files Stone had knocked onto the floor.

So Stone had picked up her bra, but before he could give it to her, she'd shouted at him to get out of her office. "Get out! Get out! Oh, my God, I can't believe we did that! That was a mistake!"

Stone couldn't have agreed more. And he hated making mistakes. But that one…with her…he hadn't minded one damn bit. In fact, he'd enjoyed the hell out of it and out of her.

She'd felt so damn good—so hot and tight.

"Mr. Michaelsen?" the judge asked from his seat on the bench. "Do you have something to say?"

And now Stone was the only one standing as everyone else had followed the judge's example and taken their seats. Heat rushed to his face, and he shook his head. As he sat down, his client looked quizzically at him, his brow furrowed.

"Are you okay?" Byron whispered.

Stone nodded. "Yeah, yeah…" He was trying to convince himself as much as his client. What the hell was wrong with him? How had he let her get to him like she had?

"Is this some weird strategy of yours?" Byron asked.

Had the man seen the bra?

Stone hadn't intended for anyone but Hillary to see it—to know that he had it, that he had had her. But now he wondered who had had whom.

He snapped his briefcase closed. "Everything's under control," he assured his client.

Now.

Last night Stone had never been more out of control than he'd been with Hillary Bellows. He didn't dare glance over at her. He could imagine how much she was enjoying this. As much as she'd enjoyed last night?

Hillary barely held in the giggle tickling her nose and throat. But she knew if she let the laugh slip out, she would be reprimanded next. And if the judge asked her why she was laughing…

She couldn't tell him the truth without uptight Judge Harrison tossing her off the case. But she wouldn't be able to lie, either. Not in court.

Damn it.

Damn Stone Michaelsen.

Why the hell had he kissed her the night before? And why hadn't she been able to resist him?

She'd known—even as she was tearing off his clothes—that it was a mistake. But she'd had to see that magnificent body of his naked. And he hadn't stopped her.

She wished now that he would have, because she couldn't unsee what she'd seen. She couldn't unfeel what she'd felt. He was even more amazing than he'd been in her fantasies. His body was perfect—all taut skin and hard rippling muscles. And the way he'd touched her, kissed her, moved inside her…

Heat flushed her body as tension wound tightly inside her. She needed him moving inside her again.

"Ms. Bellows!" The judge bellowed her name. "Are you ready to call your first witness?"

Now heat flushed her face. She jumped to her feet and said, "Yes, Your Honor, I am."

Not ready. She was not ready to think about anything but what had happened the night before. But she couldn't think about that anymore.

She couldn't think about Stone Michaelsen as anything but the opposition in court. And as the opposition, she had to crush him and now she had the evidence to do it. He was not going to help another guilty person get away with their crimes as he'd helped too many others.

She called her first witness to the stand. It was the maid who'd found the young Mrs. Mueller's body in her husband's den. She turned around to watch the woman enter the back of the courtroom. And as she turned, she saw Stone first and that damn briefcase where he'd stuffed her bra. And she remembered how he'd gotten her off the night before.

Twice.

In the bra she wore, her nipples tightened, and her core began to pulse with desire. How the hell could she want him yet? His bringing her bra to court proved that last night had meant nothing to him beyond getting something over her. A way to manipulate her.

He wanted to mess with her case. Maybe he intended to report her to the judge and get a mistrial for his client. She held her breath, waiting for his objection or for him to ask to speak to the judge in chambers.

But hell, he wouldn't bother saving her any embarrassment. He would probably announce right in open court that he'd had sex with her in her office— on her desk.

She hadn't even noticed the folders toppling over to the ground or the hard surface of the desk beneath her butt. She hadn't been aware of anything but him and how hot and sexy he was. And when he'd touched her with his mouth, teased her with his tongue.

Her body throbbed with need. She wanted him again. But that wasn't possible. The line they'd crossed could not be crossed again.

But the damage was already done.

He could tell the judge anytime what they'd done. He could ask that she be recused because he didn't think she should be prosecuting his client after they'd had sex.

What would her boss say then?

She'd be lucky if all she lost was this case. She would probably lose her job, too.

But Stone didn't say anything until it was his turn to cross-examine her witness.

And he never looked at her again.

What the hell was he up to?

CHAPTER FIVE

JUST AS HIS client was being led off to jail again, the billionaire said something ominous to Stone. "You're playing a dangerous game here."

Stone automatically glanced over to the prosecution's table. But Hillary was already gone. He turned toward the back of the court and caught just a glimpse of her bright blond hair as she slipped out into the hall. He wanted to chase after her, but members of the press, that Judge Harrison had banned from the proceedings, surrounded her now in the hall, shoving microphones in her beautiful face. And he wasn't sure he could hide from the media how he felt about her now, how he wanted her.

Then the doors swung shut again, and he lost sight of her and the reporters. And he was able to focus on his client again. "Don't worry. I've got this."

Byron Mueller tilted his head and reminded Stone, "You have a million reasons to do your best."

"I am…" Maybe not today in court. But last night…

That had been his best. Well, it had felt the best. But he'd been quick and out of control. Had Hillary enjoyed it, too? She'd seemed to, but the minute it was over, she'd vowed it would never happen again. That it was a mistake.

And given how distracted it had made him today, she was right. It had been a mistake. One that they could not repeat. Not that she would want to repeat it. She was furious with him for bringing her bra to court.

Maybe Byron was right. Maybe he was playing a dangerous game. Stone would be lucky if she only went after him in court. And she had gone after him today. She hadn't brought up the alibi yet, but she'd used other witnesses to paint Mueller's short marriage as a contentious one.

Stone had seen the concern on his client's face. No wonder Byron uttered that warning as the guards led him from the courtroom. He didn't want to go to prison for a crime he had not committed.

But Stone was not going to allow that to happen. Hillary Bellows hadn't beaten him in court yet, and she was damn well not going to beat him this time, either. And beating her again was more incentive than even the million-dollar bonus that Mueller had offered him if they won.

Hillary could not find out about that bonus. She

would think that Mueller was just trying to buy his way out of trouble. She had already convinced the judge to deny bail, because she'd argued that Mueller would use his billions to elude justice if he was allowed out before the trial.

Despite Stone's arguments to refute her claims, bail had been denied. But Stone didn't count that as a win for Hillary. Judge Harrison rarely granted bail to anyone, so it was no surprise that he'd denied it to a billionaire. He wouldn't have wanted to be accused of bias or being bribed.

But he was actually biased against Stone's client, and he was probably biased against Stone as well. As the judge was leaving the courtroom, he'd sent Stone a warning, too. It had been silent—just a glare as he'd walked away.

The courtroom was almost empty now with the day over, but Stone hesitated before closing his briefcase and taking it from the defense table. Instead, he reached into the open case, pushed aside a folder and fingered the lace of Hillary's nude bra. It was nothing like her skin, like her breasts.

He wanted to feel her again. But that wasn't going to happen. He doubted he'd be seeing her again anytime soon outside of court. She would probably make certain of that.

But he had another woman he needed to see, one he'd already stood up in order to talk to Hillary the night before. He needed to meet with Allison Mc-

Cann. The publicist was beautiful but she didn't ex-cite him like Hillary Bellows did. He'd never been attracted to her like he was to the curvy blond as-sistant district attorney. Of course, Allison McCann was all business.

Until last night, Hillary had been, too. But when he'd seen her leaning back in her chair, moaning over that chocolate, all he'd been able to think about was making her moan again. And he had—a lot.

He let the lace slip through his fingers. Then he snapped the briefcase closed. Someone was prob-ably going to shut off the lights soon. At least when he stepped into the hall, the reporters were gone.

They probably thought he'd gone out of the court-room a back way. Judge Harrison had denied them access to the courtroom—per Hillary's request, of course. But Stone didn't consider that a win for her, either. While he and his partners used the media to help with their cases, they didn't need them in order to win. Maybe that was why he hadn't rescheduled his appointment with Allison yet.

But instead of reaching for his phone, he pushed the down button for the elevator. The doors of one of the cars slid open as if it had been waiting for him. He stepped into the empty one and selected the L button. Moments later, the doors slid open to a nearly empty lobby. Only the guards stood near the entrance. One nodded at him as he walked out.

The others ignored him. They were ready to be done for the day.

But since daylight savings had gone into effect the weekend before, night came early again. It was almost dark as Stone walked down the block toward the parking garage. Despite New York traffic being a pain in the ass most of the time, Stone preferred to drive around the city. He was aggressive enough to handle the other drivers on the streets—and the pedestrians who paid no attention to the walk signs.

A chill chased down his spine, and he suppressed a shiver. It wasn't like he was nervous or uneasy. It was just cold out. A few snowflakes even fluttered down between the tall buildings. The first snow of the season, although in November it really shouldn't have been snowy yet. It melted the minute it hit the ground. He turned off the sidewalk and walked into the parking garage. The attendant didn't even glance up from the screen of the device he held.

So much for the security the place advertised. The attendant in his security guard uniform was the only human on the premises besides Stone now. He walked past several empty parking spaces as he headed toward the level where he'd left his luxury SUV. The outside of the vehicle didn't appear very luxurious anymore, though. The black paint was scuffed in several places, and there were a few dents.

Stone drove as aggressively as he fought for his

clients. That was why he'd brought Hillary's bra to court. He'd just wanted to get a little edge on her.

Instead, he'd made himself edgy. Restless. Tense…

He wanted to relieve that tension like he had the night before—inside her, her inner muscles squeezing him as she came.

A soft groan slipped through his lips.

Just as his tactic to distract her had done in court, it distracted him once again, so much so that he didn't realize that he was no longer alone in the parking garage. He didn't realize it until it was too late and something struck him hard across the back and shoulders. He flinched and whirled around to defend himself.

But when he saw who his attacker was, he had no defense. He could do nothing but chuckle.

His amusement had more anger coursing through Hillary, and she was tempted to whack him again with her briefcase. Maybe even harder this time. But before she could swing the metal case again, he jerked it from her hands. And the grin left his handsome face.

"Do you want me to press charges for assault, Ms. Bellows?" he asked her.

"Do you want me to press charges for theft?" she replied.

The corners of his mouth curved upward in another slight grin, and his gray eyes gleamed with amusement. "I haven't taken your briefcase," he said. But he had yet to hand it back to her. "So what are you talking about?"

"You know what I'm talking about," she said. But because she didn't want anyone else to know, she had pitched her voice low and uttered the words through gritted teeth.

He furrowed his brow and shook his head. "I'm not sure what you're referring to."

"You son of a bitch," she said.

Instead of taking offense at her insult, he chuckled as if he agreed with her. But then, he hadn't brought her bra to court to return it to her. Obviously.

He'd brought it to taunt her.

That was why she'd struck him with her briefcase, because she was so furious with him. "You are!"

He nodded. "I'm not arguing with you."

"That's a first," she murmured. "Arguing with me is all you do."

He stepped closer to her and lowered his head until his lips were just inches from hers. Then he said, "Arguing isn't all we do, Hillary. Not anymore…"

She shivered. But she didn't feel cold despite the cool breeze blowing through the parking structure.

"We didn't argue last night," he continued, and he lowered his head more until his lips just brushed across hers.

Hillary jerked back as heat sparked through her body and lights flashed in the garage. But it wasn't camera bulbs flashing. The press hadn't followed them like she had followed Stone to the parking garage. All the reporters had given up on waiting for Stone after court. But she hadn't.

She'd been too furious to let him go without a fight. For her bra.

But she couldn't let anyone witness her getting her underthings back from the opposing counsel in such a high-profile case. Someone would certainly report her for alleged misconduct.

But as long as she didn't let whatever had happened with Stone affect how she handled the case, she hadn't really done anything wrong. Just stupid.

Judge Harrison and her boss might think otherwise, though.

Along with the lights, she heard the sound of an engine. The lights must have just flashed because someone had started their vehicle in another part of the parking garage. Had the driver seen them?

"Open your doors!" she hissed at him.

His brow furrowed. "What?"

He'd already taken the key ring from his pocket, so she reached for the fob and clicked the unlock button. The lights flashed on his vehicle and the horn beeped. She rushed around the rear bumper, pulled open the door and jumped into the passenger's seat. Fortunately, his windows were tinted, so no one could see inside through the windows.

But Stone pulled open his driver's door and held it open, casting her in the glow of the dome light.

"Get in!" she said, nearly hissing the words at him.

He slid beneath the steering wheel and slowly—so very slowly—pulled the door shut. Then he turned toward her and said, "I'm sorry. I didn't realize you needed a ride somewhere." Then his pupils dilated, turning his gray eyes dark, and he wriggled his brows. "Unless you just need a ride."

Heat flashed through her body again, as it had when his lips had brushed across hers. But it was anger, she told herself. She couldn't want him again.

And even if she did, she couldn't give in to temptation as she had in her office. If someone saw them...

Her reputation and her career would be over. And that was probably what he'd intended all along. Her palm itched with the need to connect with his handsome face. She wanted to slap the innuendo and sexiness right off of him.

But she didn't dare touch him because that had been her first mistake last night. No. That had been her second, or maybe her third.

Her first mistake had been not calling security to throw him out the minute he'd stepped into her office. She wouldn't have even had to place a call. All she'd had to do was press the little panic button under her desk. But she hadn't even thought of it when he'd walked in; she'd thought of nothing but those stupid fantasies she had about him.

"You know why I'm here," she said. "Give it back!"

He arched a brow and leaned across the console separating the front seats. The leather was so supple and soft. And even though the car hadn't looked new on the outside, with all its scuffs and dents, it smelled new inside—the leather fresh and expensive.

"I'll give it to you," he said.

And she suspected he wasn't talking about her bra. Her pulse accelerated as excitement coursed through her. Coming up against Stone Michaelsen in court had always been exciting. But coming up against him outside of court was something else entirely.

She wasn't sure her heart could handle this much excitement. Her pulse raced with it, her heart hammering away as she remembered the pleasure he'd given her.

He was so damn good. That was his and his partners' reputations, though. They were as good of lovers as they were lawyers.

And even she couldn't argue that they were exceptional lawyers. After last night, she couldn't argue that Stone wasn't an exceptional lover as well.

"Stop it!" she warned him. "Stop playing games with me." Because she wasn't sure she could handle any more excitement.

He leaned back and widened his eyes with feigned

shock. "Who, me? Why do you think I'm playing games?"

"Taking my bra," she said, "bringing it to court. That was adolescent." She was hoping that was all it was.

"Adolescent?" he repeated and chuckled. "There wasn't anything childish about last night, Hillary."

"We acted on impulse," she said, "without regard to the consequences. So that wasn't very mature or professional of either of us."

Unless he hadn't acted on impulse. Unless it had all been premeditated on his part, and he'd come to her office in order to seduce her.

That was what she wanted to know, even more than she wanted her bra back. "Or wasn't that the case for you, Stone? Did you plan what happened between us?" She gestured toward his briefcase. "And did you take that as evidence so you could get me removed from the case?"

He and his partners didn't have reputations for just being exceptional in court and in bed. They had reputations for being ruthless as well. She'd been hearing stories about them for years, but even more recently about women they'd purposely seduced.

Was that what he'd done with her?

Just how ruthless was Stone Michaelsen?

CHAPTER SIX

HILLARY WAS RIGHT. Stone had acted like an adolescent the night before with no regard for the consequences of giving in to his impulses. When he'd brought her bra to court, he'd acted even more childishly.

His partners wouldn't believe what he'd done— and who he'd done. Of the four of them, he was the most professional. Usually.

Something about Hillary Bellows affected him as no one else ever had. Even now, his body was so damn tense that it ached. He wanted her so badly.

And she was close. He could feel the heat of her gorgeous body across the console. She should have been cold because despite it being November, she was wearing only her suit. Since it was wool, maybe she was warm enough in it. But her legs were bare beneath the hem of the skirt, which had ridden up when she'd jumped into the passenger's seat. He could see no goose bumps on her silky smooth skin, though. He wanted to reach across that console and touch her, to slide his hand up her thigh beneath that skirt to see if she was as wet and ready for him as he was for her.

His cock throbbed behind his fly, demanding release.

"Is that what you want, Stone?" she asked, her voice sharp with impatience, probably because he hadn't answered her yet.

He couldn't remember her question anymore. He could only think about how much he wanted her, how much he wanted to thrust his dick inside her. So he snapped back at her, "Yes! That's what I want."

Her.

Naked and wild like she'd been on her desk the night before. Moaning and writhing...

Screaming his name.

That was what he wanted.

She gasped. And it wasn't with the pleasure he'd given her the night before. It was shock.

"Really?" she asked, and her voice was soft and quiet now. "You want me off the case?"

He glanced up at her face and narrowed his eyes, trying to focus on the conversation. "What?"

"You want me off the case?"

"No."

"But you just said—"

"I forgot your question," he admitted. And he felt so damn adolescent now, like some horny teenager who was so distracted by the curvy cheerleader in his class that he didn't know what the hell the teacher was asking him.

She snorted. "Yeah, right…"

And maybe it was good that she didn't believe him, because then she had no idea how much she affected him. Because if she knew, he had no doubt she would use it against him, just like he'd tried using it against her today.

He flinched as he remembered how dismally that had backfired on him.

But then she leaned back in her seat and grinned. And he suspected she'd figured it out. Hell, all she'd had to do was look at his fly. His erection was straining it so much, he was surprised the zipper hadn't separated.

She chuckled. "You know you're going to lose this time."

"What?" He really needed to pay attention to this conversation. Hillary Bellows was a challenge when all Stone's faculties were functioning. But now she was downright dangerous.

Maybe that was why Byron Mueller had issued him a warning. Maybe he'd noticed that the assistant district attorney was entirely too distracting to Stone.

"That's why you want me off the case," she said. "You know you're going to lose."

He shook his head. He couldn't. Not when he was representing an innocent man. More was riding on the outcome of this trial than a million-dollar bonus. Justice was riding on it.

She swiveled toward him, and her blue eyes glittered with merriment. "That's the reason," she said. "You're afraid of me, Stone Michaelsen."

He opened his mouth to argue, like they did in court and apparently outside of it as well. But he couldn't utter the denial—maybe because there was part of him that was afraid of her, or at least afraid of how she made him feel.

Out of control.

Stone did not like to be out of control. But at the moment, his body had taken over his mind, its demands too intense to be ignored any longer.

"I'm terrified of you," he told Hillary. But he made the truth sound like a lie as he grinned and chuckled.

And the smile slid away from her face as she tensed in the passenger's seat. Maybe she'd realized then that he wasn't the only one with a reason to be afraid.

"You should be," she said. And now she sounded like the child, petulant and defiant. "I'm going to win."

He grinned. "I think it's cute that you believe that." He leaned across the console and ran his fingertips along her delicate jaw. "But then, I think everything about you is cute."

She flinched.

He knew he sounded more condescending than complimentary. But he'd meant it that way. He couldn't tell Hillary how he really felt, that she was drop-dead gorgeous and sexy as sin. Or she would know exactly how much she distracted him.

And she could use that distraction to her benefit and his detriment. All she had to do was look at him, the way she'd looked at him the night before when she'd torn open his shirt…

And he would lose all rational thought.

Hell, he was barely capable of thought right now. He just wanted to feel her: her silky skin, her breath against his lips, her body wrapping around his.

"I know I'm not your type," Hillary said. "That's why I know this is all just some sick game to you, some sneaky trial strategy."

"What makes you think you're not my type?" he asked. He wasn't aware that he even had a type. He'd always thought of himself as an equal opportunity dater—just lately, with this case on his mind, he hadn't had much opportunity to date anyone.

"You and your friends are notorious for the women you date," she said. "For the supermodels and lingerie designers and actresses."

"You've got me mixed up with my friends," he said. Not that he hadn't dated a model or two and a couple of actresses himself. But he'd never been as involved with any of them as two of his friends were now involved. He still couldn't believe that Simon and Ronan were in love.

A twinge of panic struck his heart. That was something he would never risk. Too often falling in love led to one's downfall, like it had with Byron Mueller. And Stone's mom. And pretty much every one of the clients Ronan Hall represented in their divorce.

Nope. Stone would never risk falling in love.

But lust...

He had no control over that because he'd been lusting after Hillary for a while now—even before last night.

"You shouldn't believe everything you read about me," he continued.

She arched a brow and snorted her skepticism as she sardonically said, "Really? You're not a former runaway who survived the streets of New York to make it big in the big city?"

Apparently, she hadn't believed everything she'd read about him. But that was actually the truth.

"I was talking about my love life," he said.

She snorted again. "Love?" She shook her head. "I know you're not capable of that."

He expelled a slight breath of relief. "Good."

"You're too cold and calculating to ever fall in love," she continued.

And he flinched now. "I'm cold?"

He was burning up in the small space of his little

luxury SUV. It wasn't the heat of the bodies warming up the place. It was the desire he felt for her.

She nodded.

He reached across the console now and touched her thigh where her skirt had ridden up. Her skin was as hot as his palm. "Do I feel cold to you?" he asked.

Her breath hitched, and her eyes widened with shock as they darkened with desire. "Stone…"

She said his name as a warning.

He slid his palm higher until his fingers edged under her skirt and over the silk of her panties.

And this time when she uttered his name, it was on a moan. She shifted against the leather, and he pushed aside the silk of her panties to stroke his fingers over the silk of the short blond curls on her mound.

"Stone…" She shook her head. "We shouldn't—"

He cut her off with his mouth as he covered her lips with his. He kissed her deeply, pushing her head against the leather headrest while he slid his fingers inside her. She was already wet.

He made her wetter, sliding his fingers in and out of her just like he slid his tongue in and out of her mouth. She suckled on it with her lips. And he groaned, wanting her sucking on him instead.

She made him crazy as no one else ever had. Even when he'd been a teen, he hadn't steamed up the windows of a vehicle like he was steaming up the SUV with her. Of course, when he was young, he hadn't been able to afford a vehicle.

While kissing might have been enough when he was a kid, it wasn't enough now. He needed to bury himself inside her.

Hillary gripped Stone's arms as the orgasm rocked her. He'd made her come with just his kiss and his fingers. He hadn't even taken off her clothes. Or his.

She wanted his clothes off. She wanted hers off. She was so damn hot that her hair was sticking to her forehead and her clothes were sticking to her skin. She wanted him so badly—even after that orgasm.

It hadn't been enough. She knew he could give her more—so many more.

"Don't push me away," he murmured, his voice a low growl of frustration.

He needed her, too.

So he must have found her more than cute. She intended to make sure he found her more than cute. Grateful for the tinted windows, she stripped off her suit jacket. Then she reached for the buttons on her silk blouse.

She'd had no intention of repeating her mistake with him. But for some reason she'd worn her sexiest bra. It was red, like the blouse. But she'd only revealed a peek of it—like Stone had her nude bra in court—before he pushed her fingers aside and pulled her blouse open.

Buttons pinged and glanced off the window. She didn't care. She cared only that he pushed down the cups of the bra and closed his lips around a nipple. And the tension he'd just released wound tighter and more intense inside her. He lightly nipped at her nipple with his teeth.

And she nearly came again.

She liked sex. But she couldn't remember it ever feeling like it did with Stone—so…out of control.

She clutched his head to her breast. He teased her with his tongue, with his teeth. And she did come again—a little.

"You are so damn hot," he murmured as he slid his fingers inside her again.

She wanted him just as hot for her. So she moved her hands from his hair to his neck. She jerked his tie loose and attacked the buttons of his shirt. At least one of them pinged loose and hit the dash. Then she raked her short no-nonsense nails down the sculpted muscles of his chest to the buckle of his belt.

He sucked in a breath and his body tensed. "Hillary…"

She didn't heed the warning in his voice. She unclasped his belt and unzipped his fly, freeing the erection that had already burst through the opening in his boxers. She pushed his shoulders back so that she had room to lean over the console. Then she closed her lips around the head of him.

He was too big for her to take him all in her

mouth. But she slid her lips up and down the length of him, teasing him like he'd teased her.

But before she could give him any release, he pushed his seat back, pulling himself away from her mouth. He must have pulled a condom from his wallet at some point because he quickly sheathed himself. Then he reached for her, dragging her over the console. As he did, he pulled down her underwear, dropping it somewhere.

She didn't care where—she only cared that she was suddenly straddling him with his penis easing inside her. She pushed down so that he filled her. And a moan of pleasure slipped through her lips.

Why did he feel so damn good inside her?

Then he moved, arching his hips up from the seat. But he didn't buck her off; she was holding too tightly to him, her inner muscles clutching at him while her arms clutched his shoulders.

He leaned forward and kissed her—deeply, passionately. And as his tongue slid between her lips, he thrust again and again.

She kissed him back, as crazy for him as he seemed for her. She was beyond control, beyond anything but the passion that overwhelmed her.

He moved his lips from hers, down her throat to her breasts, which were still pushed over the cups of her red bra. And he closed his lips around a nipple again, tugging gently on it. As he did, she felt the pull from her nipple to her core.

Her inner muscles convulsed as she came, screaming his name. He tensed beneath her, and his hands gripped her hips. He drove her down on him—once, twice as he yelled out his pleasure.

She collapsed against his chest, slick with sweat, beads of it trickling through the soft dark hair and over the sculpted muscles. He was so damn sexy.

It wasn't fair.

She'd had no intention of this happening ever again. This wasn't why she'd waited for him outside the courthouse. This wasn't what she'd intended.

But she forgot about her bra. Hell, she even forgot her panties. As she pulled herself off him and eased back into the passenger's seat, she hurriedly did up the buttons that were left on her blouse before tugging her jacket over her shoulders. Then she straightened her skirt and ran her fingers through her hair.

The windows were tinted so nobody could see in. But now they were so steamed up that she couldn't see out. She had no idea who might be waiting outside his vehicle.

A reporter.

The attendant who had been drawn out of his booth by all the noise they'd been making.

She couldn't be seen. But she couldn't stay with him anymore, not when she'd been tempted to lay her head on one of his broad shoulders and cuddle with him.

She didn't have time for that, even when she

wasn't trying the case that would make or break her career. Hell, he could make or break her career.

"Give me what I came here for," she told him.

"I thought I just did," he said with a ragged sigh as his chest—his glorious naked chest—continued to rise and fall with heavy breaths.

Her face heated. "That's not why I came here, and you know it."

At least she hoped he did, that he didn't think she was some clingy, needy female desperate to be with him.

He leaned back in his nearly reclined seat and closed his eyes, as if he was about to fall asleep now. So she reached for his briefcase herself.

He caught her hand before she could even try to open the clasp. "No, no, no…" he admonished her. "No looking at my trial notes."

She would love to get a peek at those. Maybe his mole would send some over to her like she or he had Byron Mueller's and the alibi witness's bank statements.

"Is this how I wound up with that evidence?" she wondered aloud. "Some woman got into your briefcase after you fell asleep on her?"

He narrowed his eyes and glared at her. But he didn't answer her question.

Was he sleeping with someone else? Or had he been and that spurned lover was his little office mole?

Hillary told herself that she only cared because

she didn't want anything messing with the trial. But she knew that was a lie. Or she wouldn't have had sex with him herself.

Twice.

And she was afraid that if she stayed inside the steamy SUV with him, they would have it again. Her gaze dropped to his lap and his cock was already beginning to swell to its enormous, aroused size.

She shook her head. "No. It's not happening again."

He grinned—that wicked grin that had her body tingling all over again. "I believe you said that before."

"I mean it!" But just so she would not be tempted, she threw open the passenger's door and hurried out of the vehicle and away from temptation. She didn't care that he might get caught with his pants down; she didn't want to get caught up with him again.

He could have her underwear, too. If he showed it to anyone, she'd just deny it was hers. It wasn't like he could get DNA ordered on it. Of course, though, given how good a lawyer he was, he might be able to.

That was a risk she'd just have to take. It was safer than having sex with him again. Because she was afraid that if she did, she risked getting addicted to it.

And to him…

But before she could slam the door shut behind her, he uttered one last taunt. "You know that won't be the last time."

She could only hope that he was wrong. And that she would win that battle, just like she was going to win the trial.

CHAPTER SEVEN

SHE WAS WINNING.

And Stone wasn't sure what the hell to do about it. She wasn't just winning the trial, either. She was winning her vow that they wouldn't have sex again.

Sure, it had only been a week. But it felt like a lifetime since he'd been closer to her than the distance between the prosecution and the defense tables. A couple of times he'd stepped close to her, so close that he'd gotten a whiff of the shampoo she used on her hair. It was something fruity, something that made his mouth water with desire to put his face in it, to breathe deep as he thrust inside her body.

He groaned and shifted on his desk chair. It was late—or early. He had no idea at the moment. He'd gone back to the office after court had ended its session at the end of Friday. But it could have been Saturday by now. He glanced toward the tall windows, but the light was dim. Maybe it was night illuminated with the city lights of Midtown.

Despite his muscles protesting the sudden movement, Stone forced himself up from his chair and walked to the window. No. It was daylight, just overcast with ominous clouds darkening the sky.

He'd been awake all night. No wonder his body ached. But it wasn't just his neck and shoulders aching from being slumped over his desk. His body ached lower.

And it ached for Hillary...

Damn her.

She was torturing him. And she knew it. Or she must. Or why did she wear those little suits of hers just a little too snug, so that the button pulled across her full breasts and so that the skirt molded against her ass.

He wanted to grab her ass. Wanted to hold it, as he drove himself inside her. He groaned at the thought of taking her like that.

But hell, he'd take her any way he could get her right now. He wanted her so badly—almost as badly as he wanted to win. But his chances of either were starting to look as dismal as that dark sky.

The bank statements hadn't been forged or fudged like the documents the mole had concocted against Ronan. Byron Mueller had transferred a hefty sum of money to his son's friend—the one the two of them had supposedly been hanging out with on Byron's yacht when the murder occurred.

While Hillary could have argued that the son

would lie for the father—especially since the father bankrolled the son's decadent lifestyle—it would have been harder for her to claim the same about the friend, if those damn bank statements hadn't turned up.

She'd nearly been gleeful when she'd presented them in court. The kid had tried to stick to his story regarding the alibi. But she'd flustered him.

Just like she'd flustered Stone. He didn't know who to believe now.

He only knew one thing for certain. That he wanted her. She was so damn exciting in court—and out of it. As fun as it was sparring with her in front of the jury, it was even more exhilarating having sex with her.

She was so damn passionate. So damn responsive...

How could she not want him anymore?

Wasn't she aching for him like he was for her? Or did she have someone else to fill in for him?

Heels clicked against the wood floor outside Stone's open door, and his pulse quickened. Was it her? Had she come to see him? To fuck him?

He turned hopefully toward the door, but his shoulders slumped when he saw who had entered his office. Allison McCann was undeniably beautiful with her pale skin and deep red hair. But she wasn't Hillary.

Whereas Hillary was full of fire and passion, Allison was cold and aloof. Some men might consider her a challenge. But Stone knew the real challenge was a woman like Hillary—one who was as passionate about winning as he was.

It was just too damn bad that she was winning now.

He uttered a weary sigh as his sleepless night weighed on him. Unfortunately, it wasn't his only sleepless night since he'd had sex with Hillary. He was exhausted.

"Hello, Ms. McCann," he greeted her, but he could not inspire any real enthusiasm to see her. "Did we have an appointment?" It was Saturday, so he doubted it.

"A few of them, Mr. Michaelsen," she replied. "But you keep canceling them."

"I don't remember rescheduling one for today." Not that he hadn't. Hillary had him so distracted he'd only just figured out what day it was and if it was day or night. So it was possible that he had made an appointment.

Her skin flushed slightly. "*You* did not."

"I did," Trev said as he strolled into Stone's office behind her.

Stone peered at his friend through eyes bleary from lack of sleep. "Funny, but you don't look like my assistant."

Trev chuckled. "Seems like you need one for this trial. And, lucky for you, I happen to be between cases of my own."

Allison glanced at him with just a flicker of an

expression. Stone couldn't be certain but she seemed faintly surprised. He wasn't. He knew Trev was just weighing which case he wanted to tackle next. He had plenty of requests for representation. But he was looking for something that excited him.

Like Stone's case excited him. Or was it just Hillary that excited him?

Unfortunately, she—and the trial—had also exhausted him. So maybe he could use Trev's help. He settled back onto his chair, trying not to flinch as his muscles protested how much time he'd already spent at his desk. He waved Trev and Allison into the chairs in front of him.

He turned toward his partner. "So you called this meeting. What's on the agenda?"

Before Trev could open his mouth, Allison spoke. "You need to do some damage control. You're losing your trial in court and in the press."

"Have you been in court?" Stone asked.

"Yes, I have attended a couple of sessions this week," she said.

He hadn't noticed her. But then, Hillary was the only woman he'd been noticing for a while now. When she was near, she totally distracted him.

"Oh" was all he managed.

"You're not arguing with her," Trev said. He'd also observed a couple of sessions.

"You know Hillary is kicking my ass." Stone was not too proud to admit it.

"Is that all she's doing?" Trev asked, his green eyes gleaming with speculation.

If the publicist hadn't been present, Stone might have admitted the truth to his friend. But they weren't alone. And he didn't want to embarrass Hillary publicly. He saved that for private. Of course, she'd been careful to not allow him any more private time with her for the rest of the week.

He nearly groaned over how much he missed her.

Then Trev chuckled. "Guess that's my answer, huh?"

"I didn't answer you," Stone reminded him.

"And that was an answer in itself."

"God, I hate lawyers." The words slipped out of Allison McCann almost as if unbidden. She looked as shocked as Stone and Trev were when they turned toward her.

"I'm sorry," she said, and her pale skin flushed with embarrassment.

Guess she hadn't meant to say that aloud—especially as Street Legal had to be one of her biggest clients, or else why would she have shown up on a Saturday?

Instead of being offended, Stone laughed. Trev had his same sense of humor and importance, and he laughed even harder.

"It's just that you—that lawyers in general," she said, "seem to find it hard to answer a question directly."

"Stone isn't always like that," Trev defended him. "He's probably the most direct one of the four of us." He turned back toward him and narrowed his eyes as he studied Stone's face. "That's why I know something's going on with him and Hillary Bellows."

"It's not," Stone replied. At least it wasn't anymore, and he doubted that she would let it go on again.

"That's good," Allison replied.

"What?" Trev asked. "You got a thing for Stone?"

She narrowed her eyes in a glare that she turned on Trev. But Stone nearly shivered from the coldness of it.

"What?" Trev asked. "I thought you liked directness."

"I like…" Allison began, "…directness…"

"Not lawyers," Stone finished for her. He could understand that. He hadn't dated any lawyers before Hillary. Not that they were dating or anything.

They were just having sex. Or had had sex.

Mind-blowing sex. Maybe that was because they were in the same profession and understood each other so well. Or maybe it was just because she was hot as hell.

Allison McCann was not hot. She was about as cold a woman as Stone had ever met, which she confirmed when she said, "Since you're not in a relationship with Hillary Bellows, you won't mind us going after her in the media."

"Going after her?" Stone asked uneasily.

"We can bring up how she is only trying this case to go after her boss's job," Allison suggested, "how her ambition blinds her to justice."

Trev nodded in agreement.

Was that true? Was that why she couldn't see that Byron Mueller was innocent? Or was that because the billionaire was starting to look damn guilty even to Stone? That was who Stone should be talking to right now. Not Allison McCann and his partner.

"I'm not so sure that's true," Stone said in Hillary's defense.

"You don't think she's ambitious?" Allison asked.

He chuckled. "Hell, yes, she is," he heartily admitted. "But she's also all about justice." She had been during every trial they'd had together, but most especially this one. Was she like Judge Harrison and just biased against billionaires? Or did she have some personal reason to not like the man?

"She's all about winning," Allison said. "And she does against everyone…but you."

Stone tensed. He hadn't realized that. He'd known she was good, but he hadn't realized just how damn good she was.

"This case is personal to her because of you," Allison said. "We can use that, too. Say that she must have a crush on you and because you've never been interested in her, she's acting like a woman scorned—bitter and resentful."

Stone laughed again. For many reasons.

There was nothing bitter and resentful about Hillary. And she knew exactly how interested he was in her.

"What?" Trev asked. "You're not liking any of this?"

He shook his head.

"Why not?" Trev asked. "Why don't you want to go after Hillary Bellows?"

He wanted to go after her—hard. He wanted to take her on her desk again. Or in his car. Or hell, maybe even on a bed. Or up against a wall.

He wanted to fill his hands with her breasts and fill her up with his—

Trev snapped his fingers again. "What the hell's wrong with you?"

Stone ran a hand, that shook slightly, over his face. "I was up all night working the case," he said. "This wasn't the best time to have a meeting."

"You want to cancel again?" Allison asked, her voice going all prissy.

"No." But it was Trev who offered the assurance. "Stone needs to get some rebuttal out there. Hillary Bellows is giving interview after interview where she makes our law firm sound like a bunch of crooks—"

"And cons," another male voice chimed in.

Stone glanced to the doorway where Simon Kramer, the managing partner, leaned against the jamb. He didn't look any happier with him than Allison Mc-Cann did.

He groaned.

"She's right," Simon said. "We need to get some rebuttal out there."

"That's not all we need to do," Stone said pointedly. He'd told Hillary about the mole when she'd come up with those bank records because he'd been hoping they were forged like the documents used against Ronan. But for some reason he hesitated about saying anything in front of the publicist.

His partners must have felt the same, for they didn't expand. But Simon nodded in agreement. He knew they needed to find the mole.

"What?" Allison asked uneasily.

Maybe she thought they were going to fire her, especially since Stone kept canceling meetings with her.

Simon stepped forward and smiled at her. "Street Legal needs to win this case."

He knew about the million-dollar bonus, and as the managing partner, money mattered most to him.

"Why don't you and I discuss those press releases?" Simon asked Allison.

Stone stood up but not because Allison also had. He stood up to protest Simon letting her bash Hillary. But before he could say anything, Simon shook his head. That was another argument Stone knew he wouldn't win.

Simon wanted to defend and protect the firm, which had been his idea all those years when they'd lived on the streets. They had all worked hard to build it but no one harder than Simon. He was obviously determined to not let anyone hurt it. The mole. Or Hillary Bellows.

Stone sighed as they walked away.

Trev stared after Allison McCann. Once Simon led her out of sight, he let out a low whistle and asked, "Why have none of us ever been with her?"

"Would you want to read the press release she'd put out when one of us ended it?" Stone asked. He was afraid of what she was going to put out there now—about Hillary.

Hillary was already furious with him over the bra thing. And the panties. He hadn't put the panties in his briefcase. But he also hadn't returned either of the items. Of course, that was her fault. She'd told security to not allow him up unless she called down and said they had an appointment.

And he knew the only reason she'd take an appointment with him was if he asked for a plea deal for his client. But that wasn't going to happen. At least not for his client.

Stone was getting just about desperate enough to

ask for a plea deal for himself—for at least one more time with Hillary. But somehow he didn't think one more time would be enough.

It had been over a week since she'd had sex with Stone in her office. But she swore she could still smell him in it—on her. She breathed deep and closed her eyes, remembering how he'd made her feel so damn needy.

Just like she felt now. She needed him, needed him to touch her, to taste her…like he had when he'd lifted her onto her desk and dropped to his knees in front of her. He'd licked and lapped at her mound before flicking his tongue over her clit. She shifted against the chair as tension built inside her. She wanted him to go down on her again, wanted him to drive his tongue and his fingers inside her.

A soft moan slipped through her lips and she reached down, needing to touch herself like he'd touched her. But before she could slide her hand beneath her skirt, like he had, her door rattled.

Excitement coursed through her, and her already taut nipples tightened more. Maybe he'd charmed his way past security again. Maybe he was as hungry to be with her as Hillary was to be with him again.

But when her door opened, it wasn't Stone standing in front of her. It was her boss.

And all her passion fled, her distaste for her boss

chilling the heat of desire she'd felt remembering how it had been with Stone. The short guy wasn't leering at her like he usually did, though.

Instead, his eyes were narrowed and he was glaring. She knew why. She'd seen the press release Street Legal had put out. Stone had waited awhile to issue one, but he'd made up for lost time.

What he'd said…

Or what he had at least authorized McCann Public Relations to say…

Anger coursed through her, chasing away that last bit of desire she'd felt for him. If he had been the one to show up in her office, she would have slapped him instead of having sex with him.

Well, she would have at least slapped him first. Or maybe after.

It had been too long since she'd been with him outside the courtroom. But even in the courtroom he turned her on, the way he argued with her…the way he looked at her.

Even though she was beating him, he looked at her with a lot less resentment than her boss was currently looking at her with. "It's not true," she told him.

"What?" he asked. "That you're not winning the Mueller trial? That's not true?"

She leaned back and smiled with satisfaction. "Oh, that's true." And she wasn't certain who was more shocked—the defendant, his lawyer or her boss.

"You didn't tell me you had evidence to disprove

Mueller's alibi." And he sounded petulant that she'd kept that information from him.

She shrugged. "It only just recently came to my attention." Thanks to Street Legal's little office mole.

Was it some ex-lover of Stone's? Or another of the partners? She could understand a woman being bitter if Stone stopped having sex with her.

But giving out the practice's secrets went beyond scorned. That was vindictive. Just like her boss.

"You should have told me the minute you got it," he said. "I would have taken the case then."

Which was why she hadn't told him.

"But I will be taking it now."

She held back her protest to offer a weak nod. "Of course, but aren't you worried?"

"What? You think I'll lose it?" He snorted derisively, but she saw the nerves flicker in his beady little eyes.

"That must be what Stone Michaelsen thinks," Hillary said. "Or else why would he have put out those lies undermining our department?"

Wilson Tremont's forehead furrowed as he tried to follow her. "You're saying he thinks you could beat him but that I can't?"

Hillary shrugged. "Of course *I* know you're the better lawyer of the two of us," she lied. "And despite that press release, there is no way I will ever have your job." That was no lie. She shuddered at the thought.

No. Stone had gotten it right that first night in her office. Well, that right in addition to all the other things he'd done right to her.

She wanted to be a judge someday. She wanted to dole out justice, not play the games her boss had to in order to keep his job. But she wasn't above playing them herself in order to keep this case.

"You've already pointed out how I know nothing about politics," she reminded him. Of course, he was wrong, but he didn't need to know that. She'd changed her last name, so nobody would know that. "And I have no interest in learning."

Except for when she ran for district judge. Then she'd employ everything she knew. And she knew a hell of a lot.

Her boss nodded. "That's right. You've said that."

"Yeah, Allison McCann and Michaelsen couldn't have lied more in that press release than they did." She rubbed her chin and acted as if she were trying to figure out why. "What could they be up to?"

She'd led him to the water, but he had to lean over and drink himself. And he did.

His face flushed as he realized what she had. Stone Michaelsen thought she was the better lawyer. "He thinks he can beat me!" He sucked in a breath as if Stone was there and had punched him.

"So you're right to take the case from me," she said, as if she agreed with his power grab. "You can prove him wrong."

Wilson stood silently in her doorway.

"You've beaten him before, right?" she asked.

And his face flushed a deeper shade of red.

She pitched her voice low as if she was confiding a secret to him. But he already knew. "I've never beaten him before, either."

But she would this time—if he and McCann hadn't fully manipulated her power-hungry boss.

"He's always pulling some last-minute trick," Hillary continued. Like seducing her...

"That must be why he and that PR firm wanted to cause the look of dissension in our office." She sighed. "Once you take the case from me, it'll look like you fell for their game."

Wilson cussed. "Then they'll be laughing at us in the media."

She sighed and nodded. "Probably. And bragging about how they played us."

"I will not have that," he said. "You're keeping this case. I'm sure you can handle whatever game Stone Michaelsen is playing."

That made one of them. She could handle anything Stone threw at her in the media or in the courtroom. But when he touched her, when he kissed her...

Game over.

He won every time.

No. She was smart to stay away from him. No matter how much she wanted him, she couldn't risk it. She was not going to lose the case or her self-control. She'd already known her career depended on her winning. Now she wondered if her heart might as well...

CHAPTER EIGHT

STONE FLINCHED AS the door closed behind him, locking him inside the Tombs just like his client. The Tombs was slang for the Manhattan Detention Complex where defendants were held awaiting trial.

No matter how many times Stone visited jail or prison, he never got used to it. Maybe that was because he'd started visiting jails and prisons when he was too young—when his parents had gone in and out of them, serving time for dealing drugs.

His mother had cried every time, apologizing and swearing that she would change her ways. But she never had. And sick of her broken promises, Stone had saved them both the trouble of her making any more.

Once they'd gotten him out of foster care, after serving another jail term, he had run away. And he'd never intended to wind up in jail like them. But here he was.

He was just visiting, though. It was his client who

might wind up staying there. Byron Mueller must have realized that as well, because he looked like hell. Maybe it was because he couldn't dye his hair and tan in jail, but he looked old, pale and fragile now.

Like a broken man…

Hillary Bellows might have broken Mueller. But she wouldn't break Stone.

"Why'd you do it?" Stone asked. "Why'd you pay the alibi witness?"

"I told you," Byron said, "I gave Scooter money all the time. He's my son's best friend. They've been friends since they were little."

"You gave him some money," Stone agreed. He'd used that argument in court to refute Hillary's claims. But now he argued her side of it, using her words. "But never that amount. That one amount is more than all the other payouts to him combined. And the timing…"

The big transfer had happened right after Scooter had come forward to the police.

He shook his head. "It looks bad."

"It's your job to fix that," Byron said. "Hell, you never should have let the prosecution get a subpoena for those records in the first place."

She hadn't needed it. Those records had been handed to her. But he couldn't admit that or Byron would fire him for sure. Stone had tried to get them thrown out, though.

The judge had ignored his request, as he'd ignored most of his requests. That was why Stone was losing— because of Judge Harrison.

Not Hillary.

As if Byron had read his mind, he said, "She's getting to you."

"What?"

"I see the way you look at her," Byron said. "It's the same way I used to look at Bethany."

Stone shook his head, unwilling to admit what he knew was the truth. Maybe he had more in common with the billionaire than he'd thought.

The older man uttered a heavy sigh. "Unfortunately, I wasn't the only one looking at Bethany that way."

"Who was he?" Stone asked. "Who was she sleeping with?"

Byron shook his head. "I don't know."

Did Hillary? Was she going to spring that on him, too? She knew Byron's young wife had had a lover. She'd used that as his motive for killing her. And it had worked well.

Her case was strong. But she was going to rest it soon and then Stone would have the chance to present his defense. But he needed help and not from those stupid press releases McCann and Simon had issued.

He needed help from his client. "If I'm going to

help you, you have to tell me everything," Stone urged him. "I know you're holding back."

On the identity of his wife's lover. And on the reason he'd paid Scooter such a large sum. Stone could have called Byron's son to the stand to back up the alibi, but Hillary would more than rattle that nervous young man. She'd destroy him on the cross-examination.

"If you're going to help me, you have to stop letting the sexy little assistant district attorney distract you," Byron said as he stood and motioned for the guard to open the door. "You think I paid Scooter a lot? I'll pay you another million—two million total—in addition to your other fees, if you prove my innocence."

That was what had convinced Stone that the man wasn't guilty. He'd never asked Stone to get him off or help him get away with murder. He'd always asked him to prove his innocence. He was innocent.

And like he'd said, Stone needed to prove it, and he wouldn't be able to do that if he didn't stop letting Hillary distract him. What was it going to take for him to finally get enough of her?

They'd had sex twice. Would it take a third time? Fourth? Whatever it took, Stone was willing to make the sacrifice. He had a case to win and two million dollars to collect.

Hillary settled onto her couch with a sigh. It was so much softer than her chair at the office. But she was still working. She had so much work to do to stay ahead of Stone.

And she was ahead of him now.

She'd rather be under him, though.

Or on top of him…

A lusty sigh slipped through her lips as she remembered how it had felt straddling him in the SUV, how deep he'd driven inside her with each thrust of his hips.

She'd never been filled so completely. But then, he was so damn big. Larger than life in every way.

Her doorbell rang, and she jumped. But she had no hope it was him. She'd been sorely disappointed the last time she'd thought he had shown up at the office, but it had only been her boss. Who was it this time?

Not Stone. He had no idea where she lived. Maybe her boss had tracked her down here. He might have figured out that she'd manipulated him, even more effectively than McCann and Stone had tried, and he intended to take the case from her anyway.

Her stomach tight with dread, she stood up and walked toward the door. Since it was the weekend yet, for a few more hours, she was dressed casually in soft knit leggings and a long sweater that hung off one shoulder. She touched her face, uncertain if she'd put makeup on or not.

But it didn't matter if she hadn't. Her visitor had shown up unannounced. So unless it was Stone—and it wasn't—she didn't care how she looked. No. She didn't care how she looked for him, either.

He'd probably think it was cute that she wasn't wearing makeup. Without it, she looked more like a teenager than thirty.

Just as the bell pealed out again, she pulled open the door. It wasn't her boss leaning against the jamb. Unfortunately, it also wasn't Stone.

No, that was fortunate. She didn't want him to know where she lived; she didn't want him in her place—even though she couldn't deny that she wanted him inside her, buried deep.

"Hey, remember me?" her visitor asked, and Dwight's mouth curved into a sheepish smile.

She didn't step back; she didn't want him inside—her apartment or her. "I thought you had a girlfriend."

He snorted. "That was a mistake—trying a relationship. What we have works better." He stepped closer.

He was tall like Stone. But unlike Stone, he was thin instead of muscular. His hair blond instead of black, and it was already thinning despite Dwight being the same age as she was.

"Why does it work better?" she wondered aloud.

"Because it takes less effort."

Maybe she should have been offended. But she understood. Neither of them had time for complicated and feelings and…

Whatever the hell Stone made her feel. She sure as hell didn't have time for that.

She didn't have time for Dwight now, either, because it was clear he hadn't shown up because he wanted to be with her. It was obvious he wanted to be with someone else—someone who'd required more effort from him.

"I'm busy right now," she told him. She was resting her case in the morning. She had to make sure she hadn't missed anything, that she hadn't given the jury any cause to let Stone give them a reasonable doubt.

He glanced over her head into her living room. "Do you have someone here?" he asked. "Are you seeing someone?"

She laughed at the thought of her being in a relationship. Like she would ever have the time or the energy for that. She knew relationships were fleeting and not worth the effort and definitely not worth the pain when they ended. And they always ended for one reason or another.

A noise behind Dwight drew her attention. It was the sound of someone clearing his throat. As Dwight turned to see who was coming down the hall, he stepped back against the wall with its faded brocade wallpaper. And Hillary saw Stone round the corner of the corridor.

How long had he been standing back there, out of sight but not earshot?

Hillary felt another laugh bubble up in her throat. But she was afraid it might sound hysterical if she let it slip out. So she swallowed it down.

Dwight recognized Stone and held out his hand. "Mr. Michaelsen, it's an honor to finally meet you."

Stone stared at his hand for a long moment before clasping it tightly. So tightly that Dwight flinched. "We haven't actually met," he pointed out. "Who the…?" He swallowed hard as if choking down a curse. "Who are you?"

"Dwight Hanson," her friend told Stone with all the eagerness of a little boy meeting his sports idol.

She hadn't realized Stone was an idol to anyone. But it stood to reason that he might be to an ambitious lawyer like Dwight who struggled with making commitments. Of course, Dwight would envy Stone's legendary success in the courtroom and the bedroom.

"I work at Swanson and Turner," Dwight said. "I have cited so many of your cases when I've been arguing mine."

"How's that worked out for you?" Stone asked.

Dwight's pale skin flushed. "Well, the judges have pointed out that I'm not you."

Hillary didn't need a judge to point that out to her. But it had never been more obvious than it was now when the two men stood side by side.

"Still, it's a gutsy move to use my court cases in your arguments," Stone acknowledged.

Dwight beamed with pride that he'd received a compliment from his idol. "Thank you so much for that. I'd love to talk to you more about the Rapier murder trial. It didn't seem like there was any way Rapier wasn't going to prison for the rest of his life."

"He should have," Hillary said. That was one of the cases she'd lost to Stone, one that still bothered her. Stone had used battered-husband syndrome in his defense. Rapier's wife had been abusive but she still hadn't deserved to die—as Stone had implied.

"He'd already suffered enough through twenty-five years of marriage to a person who physically and mentally and emotionally not just abused but destroyed him, his spirit, his soul, his will to even live," Stone said, repeating a line verbatim from his closing argument.

Hillary glared at him while Dwight applauded. "That was amazing."

"Thank you," Stone said and lowered his head in a slight bow.

Hillary considered telling them to get a room and closing her door. But it was so good to see Stone, especially as he was now. Like her, he wasn't wearing a suit. He was dressed casually in jeans and a soft silvery-gray cashmere sweater that nearly matched his eyes. Or it would have had his eyes been the lighter color they usually were. But they were dark now, the pupils dilated as he looked away from Dwight and focused on her.

"Oh, I'm sorry," Dwight said. "You must be here to talk to Larry."

"Larry?" Stone repeated and peered around Hillary as if expecting that she had another man inside her apartment already.

She nearly laughed again at the expression on his face. His skin flushed, and his nostrils flared. It was almost as if he was jealous. But that was ridiculous.

"We've called Hillary that since law school," Dwight said. "There's nothing girlie about her."

Well, so much for Stone being jealous.

He turned back toward Dwight and arched a brow as if incredulous. "Are you blind, man?" he asked him. "Everything about her is girlie."

Now she was offended. "What?"

Dwight snorted. "Sure, she looks like a girl, but she fights like a man."

And that was why she and Dwight were friends. It wasn't just for the uncomplicated sex. It was because he understood her.

"She hits below the belt," Stone agreed.

"And she'll do anything to win," Dwight said. And as he said it, he glanced back and forth between them. His brow puckered as if he was wondering how far Hillary had already gone with Stone.

Too far.

Too damn far…

CHAPTER NINE

STONE WAITED FOR the guy to get the picture and walk away. But he lingered yet in the hallway, as if he expected to stay and for Stone to leave. He was not going anywhere, though. And he was damn well not going to let this guy stay, either.

"So you're just friends?" Stone asked him.

"Good friends," Dwight Whatever replied. And there was innuendo in his voice. He was more than just a friend, and he wanted Stone to know that.

The blond guy turned toward Hillary now, and his voice lowered to an almost desperate plea. "I really need to talk to you, Larry."

She sighed and shook her head. "I don't think I'm the one you need to talk to."

"But that's complicated, and you and I don't do complicated." He glanced at Stone, though, and it was in his gaze and in his voice—the warning so many people had given Stone was being given to Hillary now.

Her good friend was warning her that it was too complicated for her to get involved with Stone.

Hillary didn't need any reminder of that; she was well aware and that was why she'd banned Stone from her office. She obviously hadn't counted on him finding her home, which was understandable since it hadn't been easy for him to manage. It had taken him almost the whole damn week.

He'd lost enough time tracking her down. He didn't intend to waste another minute on this guy. "I need to talk to Hillary," Stone said.

Dwight didn't budge from the doorway. "About the trial?" he asked, but he was clearly skeptical because he added, "Shouldn't that be done at the court-house or in your offices?"

"Haven't you been a lawyer long enough to know that's not how things always get done?"

"So you're here to ask for a plea?" Hillary asked, and her lips curved into a triumphant smile.

"You know why I'm here," he said. And it wasn't to plead for his client. He wanted to plead for him-self, for one more time.

At least…

Her blue eyes darkened, and her face flushed.

"You're losing this one," Dwight said, and what-ever hero worship he'd been showing Stone was gone now.

Stone only spared him a glance. All his attention was on Hillary now.

Always…

That was the problem. That was probably why he was losing. His client was right to be worried. Stone needed to focus on the case, but he couldn't do that until he relieved some of this tension inside him.

He could have called someone else. Hillary apparently might have. No. It sounded like Dwight had shown up on his own.

But if Stone hadn't arrived when he had, would she have already let dopey Dwight inside? Not just her apartment but her body?

The thought sent some strong feeling coursing through him—so intense that he clenched his hands into fists. It wasn't just anger. Anger he could control. This was stronger than that and had Stone stepping closer to the thinner man.

While his partners had used their charm and brains to survive on the streets when they were all teen runaways, Stone had used his size. Sometimes the brains and the charm had taken too long. Size was instant intimidation that usually had people backing down.

Dwight backed down. Actually, he backed up against the wall behind him. Then he looked to Hillary as if imploring her to help him.

Maybe he thought Stone would leave if she told him to. But even if she did, Stone wasn't going anywhere. He'd worked too hard to find her. He was, at the least, going to talk to her. But he wanted more than that. He needed more than that.

He needed her. She was the woman he wanted. Maybe it was because of the trial—because the heat of their arguments fueled the heat of their passion.

Once the trial was over, maybe whatever was between them would cool off. Or go away completely. He hoped that was the case.

He didn't want complicated any more than Hillary and Dwight. And it couldn't get much more complicated than this thing with Hillary already was.

She hadn't said anything yet, so Dwight implored her, "Tell him to leave."

"You're the one who needs to leave," Stone said. And he stepped closer until the guy was pressed entirely flat against the wall. "Now!"

Finally, Hillary moved from her doorway and grabbed Stone's arm, tugging him back. "What's wrong with you?" she asked.

Dwight had enough space now to ease from between the wall and Stone. He moved down the hall to where it curved around the bank of elevators. "Man, you must really hate to lose," he bitterly remarked to Stone.

"You're the one leaving," Stone pointed out. So he was the one losing.

Dwight must have realized that because disappointment flashed in his eyes just before he literally turned that corner.

And Stone figuratively turned a corner. He went from the suave, cultured lawyer he had become back to the street kid who was always ready to fight.

Dwight was gone, so he turned toward Hillary. She was usually always ready to fight, too. And as if she'd read his mind, she swung her hand and slapped his shoulder.

"What the hell's wrong with you?" she asked again. "Why are you acting like a Neanderthal?"

"Because I am one," he admitted. "You think it's just a press release, but I was once a teenage runaway."

She narrowed her eyes with suspicion. "Really? I know for a fact that not all your press releases are factual."

"Not the last one," he admitted. He knew she had no interest in her boss's job. "But you are all about winning—your *good* friend just said so."

He barely knew Dwight, but he hated the guy— hated that he'd touched her like Stone wanted to touch her again. *Needed* to touch her.

"And from living on the streets," Stone continued, "I learned that I had to fight for what I wanted."

"What do you want?" Hillary asked, and her usually strong voice sounded breathless.

She *knew*.

But he told her anyway. "You!" Then he pulled her into his arms. Her feet dangling above the floor, he walked her backward into her apartment and kicked the door closed behind them.

"I didn't—"

Whatever she'd been about to say was lost when his mouth covered hers. He'd been so hungry for her for so long that he kissed her deeply, with all the emotion coursing through him. He didn't recognize that first one—that one had been more intense than anger—because he'd never felt it before.

But he felt it again as he thought of Dwight coming here to be with Hillary. And he wanted to brand her as his.

He'd never felt such a primitive urge before. It was even more intense than when he'd lost control the first time they'd had sex. But just like then, she matched his passion.

Her fingers clutched his hair. But she didn't pull him away from her. She held his head to hers as she kissed him back. Her desire was in her lips as they moved hungrily over his, in her tongue as it darted inside his mouth to taste him. Then she ran her hands over his sweater, molding the cashmere to his chest before she tugged on the hem to pull it up.

He stepped back, just enough so that he could drag off his sweater. Then he reached for hers. It had already fallen off one shoulder, leaving it bare but for the thin strap of a black bra. He tugged the sweater off and unclasped her bra so that it dropped to the floor, too.

Then he pushed down her pants and the little scrap of lace she wore beneath them. He had to have her now.

She reached for his belt, jerked it loose and lowered his zipper, metal hissing. His breath hissed, too, out between his clenched teeth, as she touched him, her fingers stroking over the head of his engorged cock.

He was too close to the edge. So he pulled her hand away. His was shaking as he fumbled for a condom and tore it open. He rolled it on quickly before he lifted her up and eased inside her.

She locked her legs and arms around him, clutching him as she moved. She was as desperate for release as he was, and for him as he was for her.

He turned her so that her back leaned against her front door. And he took her right there, just inside her apartment. He took her in a frenzy of need.

And not just for release.

He needed to be with her on a more elemental level, as if he was claiming her as his. He lowered his head and kissed her breasts, moving his mouth over the fullness of one before closing his lips over a nipple. He nipped at it gently with his teeth, and she cried out.

But it wasn't in pain. She bucked and writhed in his arms, arching her hips as she slid up and down him.

Her inner muscles convulsed, squeezing him as

she came, screaming his name. And his name on her lips snapped the last of his control.

He thrust again and again until his body tensed, then shuddered as a powerful release overtook him. He came and came…like he had never come before.

And when it was over, his knees shook, and he felt a fear like he hadn't felt since he'd been living alone on the streets—before he'd found the other guys. No. He felt even more vulnerable than he had then. Back then he'd been afraid of losing his life.

Now he was afraid of losing his heart.

"What the hell was that?" Hillary asked as Stone stepped out of the small bathroom. Like her, he'd dressed again. He must have even splashed some water on his face because a droplet dripped off his rigid jaw.

Or maybe it was sweat. Hillary's skin was damp beneath her sweater. She felt flushed yet, hot. And despite that release that had turned her muscles— the few she had—to mush, she wanted him again.

He looked so damn handsome, even with his jaw clenched and his brow furrowed. He seemed as frustrated as he'd been when he'd shown up at her door.

"I don't know," Stone said.

And she believed he was being honest. He had no idea. And neither did she. What was it about him that affected her so much, that made her want him? Even now, after that mind-blowing orgasm, she wanted him again. But she wanted some answers first. "Why are you really here?"

"After that, you need to ask?"

"You don't need me for that," she said. "I'm sure there are slews of women who would be happy to have sex with you." Desperate even. And she'd vowed not to become one of those women. But anytime they were alone together she forgot that vow, forgot what a bad idea it was to have sex with opposing counsel in the biggest trial of her career.

"Is that why *Dwight* was here?" he bitterly asked. "For sex with you?"

He sounded so pissy that she couldn't help but smile. "Jealous?" she asked.

His eyes widened as if the thought hadn't occurred to him. But then, given his life, the way women threw themselves at him and his partners, he'd probably never had a reason to feel jealous before.

But he shook his head. He was either in denial or too proud to admit the truth. "I just want to know what the hell you have with that guy," he said. "The same thing you have with me?"

She'd never had with anyone else what she had with Stone. But she wasn't about to admit that to him. "*We* don't have anything," she told him, "except a trial in common."

He stepped closer to her and called her on the lie. "Bullshit. You know we have more than that—we have this…" He leaned down and kissed her, driving his tongue inside her mouth like he'd driven himself into her body. When he pulled away, they were both panting for breath. "You don't have that with skinny little Dwight," he said. "You can't."

"I can't have anything with you," she said. "Not when we're both on this trial." Maybe she shouldn't have talked her boss out of taking the case from her. It was what Stone had wanted, but she didn't think it was because he wanted to publicly date her.

He only wanted sex with her. Not a relationship. And that was all this was: sex. And she wouldn't let that—or anything else—affect how she handled the trial.

His lips curved into that slight wicked grin of his. "How the hell did you talk Wilson Tremont out of taking it away from you?"

"I pointed out it's what you want," she said. "Because you think you can beat him. You know you're going to lose to me."

He shook his head. "If you get a conviction, the one who's going to lose is Byron Mueller," he said. "He's innocent."

She laughed. "How can you say that? I've pretty much presented my whole case, and there's overwhelming evidence showing that he did it. He killed his wife."

But Stone just stubbornly shook his head again. "No, he didn't."

"The only thing you had to prove his innocence was that fake alibi," she said. "And those bank records blew that up. You're going to lose."

That was probably what was wrong with him—just like Dwight had suggested. He really hated to lose—probably because he'd done it so rarely. If ever...

She wasn't sure if he'd ever actually lost a case. Usually if it looked like he wasn't going to win, he pleaded them down to lesser charges.

"You wouldn't have those records if not for that damn office mole," he muttered as he glanced around her apartment. It was small. The hall opened onto a tiny living room that doubled as the dining room with a kitchen in a corner of it. There was one other door off the hall and that was to her bedroom. She wasn't letting him in there, though.

She shouldn't have let him inside at all. And she definitely shouldn't have had sex with him.

"You wouldn't have turned them over?" she asked.

"*I* didn't have them," he said.

She wasn't sure if she believed him. He'd already proved that he would do anything to win: even her. But she wasn't throwing this trial just because she was starting to have...

What?

What was she starting to have for him?

Feelings?

A chill chased down her spine, and she shivered

despite the heaviness of her sweater. No. It wasn't possible. She had vowed long ago to never fall in love with anyone. She knew all relationships eventually ended, or one person let the other person down.

She didn't want to get hurt.

Again...

CHAPTER TEN

THE WAY HILLARY was staring at him was the same way she stared at a hostile witness—just before she broke him, like she'd pretty much broken Byron's alibi witness, Scooter. He rubbed a hand around the back of his neck. Despite that soul-shattering release, he was still tense. Still edgy.

And it wasn't just because of the way she was looking at him. It was because of the way she made him feel: out of control. Stone did not like that at all.

"It was a mistake coming here," he murmured.

"So you're not going to ask for a plea deal for your client?" she asked, and she arched a blond brow.

She knew that wasn't why he'd come to see her. "I don't plea out for an innocent client."

She snorted. "There's nothing innocent about Byron Mueller. Or you."

"I told you I didn't know about those bank records," he said. And he was getting damn sick of defending himself.

"The envelope had the logo and address for Street Legal," she said. "It came from your office."

"The mole has access to our stationery somehow," he said. The documents forged about Ronan had been on their stationery as well.

"So it's someone who works for you," she surmised.

He and his partners had deduced the same thing and had even identified a suspect. But Simon's former assistant, Bette Monroe, wasn't guilty of anything but making Simon fall in love with her.

Stone considered that a crime, though. Falling in love was too dangerous. It was what had caused his mom to turn to the same life of drugs as Stone's father. She'd used and sold just to make her husband happy. If not for him, she would have never tried them. If not for him, she would have gotten clean. But she'd been more addicted to his father than she'd been to the drugs.

There was no way she would have ever left him— if she hadn't overdosed some years ago. At least that was what Stone had heard from the private investigator he'd hired to look for his parents.

Fingers snapped in his face, and Stone focused on Hillary. Her blue eyes were soft with concern, and she asked, "Are you okay?"

He sighed and nodded. "Yeah."

"What's really bothering you?" she asked. "Your office mole or the fact that you're losing this trial?"

You. She was what was really bothering him,

making him think about things he hadn't thought about in years. Like his past. Like his parents...

"I am not going to lose," he insisted. He couldn't. Not when he had an innocent client. "The truth will come out."

"It already has," she said. "You just refuse to accept it. Old moneybags Mueller killed his child bride in a fit of jealous rage."

Stone snorted. "Jealous rage over what?"

"Her lover."

"Rumored lover," Stone said. "You presented no proof this person actually exists. Just speculation from the staff and her friends."

"Speculation would have been inadmissible," she said with a smile. "I had eyewitness accounts that Byron found out about the lover and was enraged."

He shrugged like he didn't believe her. But during his last meeting with his client, he'd gotten the impression that Byron did know she'd had a lover and who that lover was. "I'm well aware you presented that as your motive. But you're wrong," he said. "This was no crime of passion."

She stepped closer to him then and said, "You're right about Dwight. We're more than friends. We hook up whenever we're between relationships and bored."

He'd known it, but her saying it put images in his head, images of her wrapped around that little skinny lawyer like she'd been wrapped around him moments ago. And once again his control snapped, and he dragged her up against him.

Before he could utter the word burning in his brain, she laughed and saved him from making a fool of himself. Because the word he'd been about to say was *Mine*.

Stone released her so abruptly that Hillary stumbled back and nearly fell. And her laughter stopped. He looked shocked. Maybe she'd finally gotten through to him.

"You get it now," she said. "You understand how a man could become so jealous that he might commit a crime of passion."

Stone shook his head. "I'm not jealous."

But the words rang hollowly. She was tempted to mess with him again, like she had earlier. But before she could say anything more, he continued.

"And men get jealous all the time without ever killing anyone over it," he said. "If Mueller had found out his wife was cheating on him, he would have just divorced her."

She snorted. "And lose any of his millions?"

"Billions," Stone corrected her.

She'd seen the bank records; he wasn't exaggerating. But she hadn't been impressed. She knew someone who had more money and wasn't as obnoxious about it as Byron Mueller. "Exactly."

Stone snorted now.

"I know he has some money to spare," she said. "But men like Mueller don't like giving up any of that money, especially to a woman who's wronged him."

"He wouldn't have had to give up a dime," Stone said. "My partner Ronan Hall drew up an ironclad prenup before Byron married his latest bride—"

"Late bride," Hillary corrected him. "She's dead."

"But my client wouldn't have killed her," Stone insisted, "even if he found out she was cheating. He would have just divorced her."

Damn it! Stone was good—so good that he was getting to Hillary. And she could not have that, could not have him swaying her, because if he could sway her, he would definitely sway the jury.

"Sure," she agreed. "If he was thinking rationally, you're right. He would have just divorced her. But in the heat of the moment, finding out that she was cheating on him…" She stepped closer to Stone and ran her fingertips over the cashmere that was molded to the sculpted muscles of his chest. They rippled beneath her touch, and his heart began to beat harder. She could feel it as she laid her palm over it. "…finding out that she was with another man, kissing him…"

She leaned closer and brushed her mouth across his throat, and his pulse jumped beneath her lips. "Touching him…" She skimmed her hand down his chest to the buckle of his belt, then lower, over his fly…

"Damn you!" he cursed her on a raspy breath. And

he reached for her again. But he didn't just jerk her against him. He swung her up in his arms. "Where's your bedroom?"

She laughed again as she pointed out the door to him. It was painted white like the walls and the scarred wood floor. "See what I'm saying," she said. "Passion…"

"You going to pull that in court to prove your point?" he asked as he turned to get her and his broad shoulders through her doorway. "You going to get every member of the jury all worked up and jealous?"

"Do you think it would work?" she asked.

He dropped her onto the bed so that she bounced against the mattress. Just like Dwight had warned him, her bedroom wasn't girlie. Hillary was not girlie. So there was nothing pink or floofy. Her room was white, like the rest of the apartment. Her sheets were white, too, with thin blue pinstripes on them. But her bed was unmade, and the only pillows were the ones she slept on.

But Stone didn't seem to mind a bit. He pulled off his sweater, his muscles rippling in his chest and washboard abs. "Worked on me…"

So he was all worked up and jealous…

Over her?

She never would have imagined that in a million years before that night in her office, when he'd kissed her. That had just been a little over a week ago, but it felt like a long time.

So long that she couldn't remember a time that she hadn't wanted him. But then, even before that night, she'd wanted him—had had her little hot fantasies about him.

If he was truly jealous about Dwight, she could have told him that the last several times she'd been with the other man, she'd imagined that he was Stone.

She'd wanted him to be Stone.

Why was she so damn attracted to a man like him? One who represented criminals and killers? And he didn't just represent them; he got them off.

That wasn't going to happen this time, though. This time she was going to win.

After stripping off his clothes, he reached for hers. He dragged off her sweater, tousling her hair. Then he peeled her pants and underwear down her legs. And as he did, he kissed every inch of skin he exposed. His lips skimmed over the arch of her foot and her ankle before moving up her calves and thighs to her core.

And then he teased her with his mouth until she was the one all worked up. She clutched her sheets in her hands as she writhed around on the mattress. The tension was wound so tightly inside her that she thought she might break. Then he flicked his tongue across her clit and slid his fingers inside her, and she did break, shattering into a million pieces as she came.

Shuddering with the release, she sank back against the bed. But then he was there, covering her limp body with his. The hair on his chest brushed across her nipples, making them tighten into sensitive peaks. And the tension wound inside her again. Despite that shattering release, she wanted him again. But he continued to tease her, just brushing his body against hers and his lips across her lips.

She wanted him as out of his mind as he was making her. So she touched him back, gliding her fingertips over every perfect inch of his body.

He groaned and cursed her as he reached for his jeans and grabbed another condom from a pocket. A muscle twitched along his tightly clenched jaw as he rolled it on. Then he eased himself inside her.

She tightened her inner muscles, pulling him deep.

And he groaned again. "You're driving me crazy!"

She could relate. He did the same to her. And she must have lost her mind to have let him into her apartment and now her bed. But she wasn't about to kick him out when she needed him so badly.

"Stone…" She raked her nails down his back to his butt, urging him to thrust harder, deeper.

Instead, he drew out. "What?" he asked, but his voice was so rough with passion it was barely recognizable. While he was teasing her, he was not unaffected himself. "What do you want, Hillary?"

"You!" She arched her hips and wrapped her legs around him. "I want you!"

Her confession seemed to snap his control. For he moved again, sliding in and out of her. And he lowered his head, kissing her deeply.

Until Stone—until experiencing the passion she felt with him—Hillary had never really understood crimes of passion. But as her tension broke and her body shuddered with the force of the orgasm Stone had given her, she understood why someone might kill to feel like this, the way only he had ever made her feel.

His body tensed, then shuddered, too, as his tension broke. He leaned his forehead against hers as he panted for breath. And he cursed her again.

And she knew that she had won this argument.

But what would happen once she won the trial? Would she and Stone never do this again? Never see each other again? Never feel this way again?

She didn't feel like such a winner now—when she considered all that she might lose with winning.

CHAPTER ELEVEN

"What's the deal?" Simon asked.

Confusion had Stone furrowing his brow as he peered across the conference table. "Deal?" They weren't playing poker. This was their weekly Tuesday morning meeting in Simon's office, sunlight streaming through its tall windows.

"Hillary Bellows rested the prosecution yesterday," Simon said.

And she'd rested it so well that Stone was beginning to have doubts of his own about his client's innocence.

"So what's your plan to tear apart her case?" the managing partner asked.

"No more untrue press releases," Stone told him. He didn't mind playing dirty with Hillary—but that was in the bedroom, not the courtroom or in the media.

Simon sighed. "I can't believe that didn't work."

Clearly dumbfounded, Ronan Hall shook his head

as well. "Can't believe Wilson Tremont's enormous ego didn't have him snagging the case from her right away."

"She got to him," Stone said. "Made him afraid that he would lose." Just like she was beginning to get to him. Stone wasn't afraid of losing for his own sake, though. He was afraid of losing for an innocent man.

Byron Mueller was innocent. Wasn't he?

Damn Hillary...

She was making him doubt his client. But that wasn't all she was making him doubt. She was making him rethink every decision he'd ever made from who he represented to how he lived his life—solitarily. But for these guys...

They were his closest friends. And as his closest friends, they jumped to his defense.

"Wilson Tremont would definitely lose," Ronan said. "The guy's an idiot."

"Too bad she got to him," Trevor remarked. Then he focused on Stone, his green eyes narrowed with suspicion. "Looks like she got to you, too."

What? Did he have it written all over his face how much he wanted his opposing counsel?

"I don't know what you're talking about," Stone bluffed.

But Trevor called him on it. "Bullshit!"

And Simon added, "Don't try to con a con. What's going on with you and Hillary Bellows?"

Even as heat rushed to his face, Stone shook his head in denial. "What makes you think—"

"You didn't want to go after her," Simon said. "You haven't played as dirty as you usually would."

They had no idea how dirty he'd played with Hillary Bellows. But something must have flickered in his eyes, some glimmer of desire over all the ways he'd been dirty to and with Hillary, because Ronan laughed.

More heat rushed to his face. "What?"

"You and the hot ADA!" Ronan exclaimed. "Way to mix business with pleasure, bro!"

"I…" He couldn't deny it. He'd never known pleasure like what he felt with Hillary.

Trevor shook his head and sighed.

"What?" Stone repeated.

"Et tu, Brute," Trev dramatically murmured.

"I didn't betray you." But he felt like he might have betrayed his client. He'd been so distracted by his attraction and passion for Hillary that he hadn't defended him as best as he should have.

Trev just shook his head and uttered a sigh of disappointment. "I didn't think you would ever fall."

"I haven't," Stone insisted. "I'm not in love with her." He couldn't be. It wasn't possible. He'd vowed long ago to never make himself that vulnerable to another human being, like his hapless mother had been.

"Then why the hell are you risking your case to have sex with her?" Simon asked.

He could have denied that, too. But these were his friends. He didn't lie to his friends, even though he suspected he was lying to himself. "I'm not risking my case," he insisted.

"You're not going after her like you normally would," Simon insisted.

Simon had no idea how much Stone had gone after her, how hard he'd taken her. But she matched his passion every time. She was incredible.

Such an amazing lover and lawyer.

"She's made a compelling case," Stone said. "Thanks to our damn office mole giving her those bank records."

They all cursed then in unison.

"I wonder where the hell they found them," he continued. Because he'd never seen them. "And my client isn't being completely honest with me," he added. Then he flinched as he played back what he'd just said inside his head and heard all the excuses he was making. He sighed. "None of that is the real issue, though."

Simon arched one of his blond brows as he usually did. "What's the real issue?"

"I need to make a stronger case." For his client and for himself.

He needed to protect them both.

"We've got your back," Simon said—just as he'd told them all so many years ago when they'd met up on the streets of the city. They'd been so alone and desperate then.

Stone hadn't felt like that since meeting them—until the other night when he'd been so desperate to see Hillary, to be with Hillary.

And he worried that it might already be too late for him to protect himself. But he'd made a promise to his client, and that one he would not break.

Hillary looked down at the witness list Stone had given her. He intended to call his client. That was crazy—even for him. Defendants rarely took the stand in their own trials. But then, that often made juries think them even guiltier when they wouldn't.

Was that Stone's strategy? To make his billionaire client more accessible? More relatable?

He'd done that with Ernest Rapier. And every juror had cried along with the man whose wife had tortured him for more than two decades. Even Hillary had had to blink away tears before they slipped out. But she knew she wouldn't be tempted to cry for Byron Mueller.

The guy was brash, belligerent and in your face. And she couldn't wait to get in his face.

And Stone was giving her the opportunity to do that, to tear apart Byron Mueller on the stand.

Knuckles brushed against her closed door. And she tensed. Hopefully, it wasn't her boss. She couldn't let him take this case now, not when she was so close to getting a conviction. He wouldn't be able to do what she would to Byron; he'd be too afraid of the political consequences of making an enemy of the billionaire.

She would use that to manipulate him this time; she would use his own ambitions against him. So she pasted a smile on her face and called out, "Come in."

The door slowly creaked open, but it wasn't her boss standing there. Stone stood in the doorway, and he looked almost sheepish. "Are you sure?" he asked. "I don't have an appointment."

"And yet no security guard called to ask me if it was okay to send you up anyway." Was there a female one on duty today? She could see him sweet-talking a woman into letting him through. Or had he been allowed up because the guard whose grandson he'd represented was working?

He glanced at his watch. "Actually, I have an appointment with your boss."

She tensed and narrowed her eyes. "Really?"

"No." He flashed a triumphant grin, his gray eyes sparkling. "But he didn't have an order out to not let me upstairs."

She reached for her phone. "Let me fix that." But she had no intention of calling her boss.

And Stone knew it, because he didn't even try to stop her from dialing.

So she dropped the phone back onto its cradle.

He quirked a brow. "Change your mind?"

"Just remembered he's out of the office." And she probably wasn't lying. It was after hours, so he had to be gone by now, probably to some function where he could kiss the ass of everyone who might help him achieve his political aspirations. She hoped he'd brought along some lip balm.

"What?" he asked, and he grinned at the look that must have crossed her face.

So she enlightened him and he laughed heartily. "You work for a jerk."

She sighed. "I know. But I didn't vote for him."

Stone shook his head. "Me neither. You going to run?"

"You believing your own press?" she asked. "I have no intention of ever doing that."

"You should," he said. "You'd be good."

She shrugged. "I'd sooner consider that bench-thing you mentioned."

"Doling out justice." He nodded. "That sounds more like you. You'll get a worse reputation than Judge Harrison has for being a hard-ass, though."

"Hey, I like Judge Harrison." At least she did when she was trying a case where Stone was representing the defendant—because Judge Harrison did not like Stone.

"Bullshit," he said.

She laughed. "Just because he's not a fan of yours…"

"I'm not a fan of his, either," Stone said. And for a moment, a look crossed his face, one of such sadness that Hillary jumped up from her chair and came around her desk.

"Are you okay?" she asked.

"Yeah, yeah, fine."

"What is it?" she asked. "Do you have a personal history with Harrison?" She forced herself to chuckle, even though that emotion she'd teased him about feeling the other night rushed over her. Jealousy. "Did you date his daughter?"

Judge Harrison was considerably older than them, even older than her boss.

"…or granddaughter?"

Stone shook his head. "No. He presided over a few cases with people I knew a long time ago."

"Who?" she asked.

He glanced at her and then away again. "My parents."

She gasped. "They were criminals?" That might explain why he'd chosen to represent them instead of making sure they were brought to justice. "But you said you really were a teen runaway."

"That was why."

"You ran away from a foster home or relatives?" she asked. And she remembered a few moments she'd thought of running away. But she'd had no place to run.

"I ran away from my parents," he said. "The lives they chose to lead, selling and using drugs."

She gasped again, feeling like something had

squeezed her heart. She wanted to reach for him, throw her arms around him and offer comfort. But she wasn't sure she knew how to do that when it had never really been shown to her.

But he saved them both the trouble when he stepped back, unwilling to accept her sympathy.

He shrugged. "Hey, it's no big deal. I don't hold any grudges against Harrison. It all worked out for the best for me. I'm doing great."

"Not in this trial," she couldn't help but add.

He mock-grimaced at her remark. "You presented your side. Now it's my turn. Everything's going to turn around," he insisted. But she couldn't help but think he was trying to convince himself as much as he was her. "You'll see."

She gestured at the list on her desk and shook her head. "I don't think so." Byron Mueller was no Ernest Rapier, but she caught herself before she changed Stone's mind about putting him on the stand.

"The jury will hear what I do when Byron talks about his wife's murder."

"Guilt?" she asked. "Remorse?" They would hear that once she got done cross-examining the witness.

Stone shook his head. "They'll hear that he had nothing to do with it."

She was almost convinced that that was what Stone believed. Maybe he wasn't just determined to win for the sake of the win. Maybe he really believed his client was innocent.

She narrowed her eyes and studied his face. "You actually think he's innocent."

"That's what I've been telling you this entire time," he said.

He had. But she'd been sure he was lying.

"So, okay," she said. But she was only humoring him. "If not your client, who killed her?"

CHAPTER TWELVE

STONE SUCKED IN a breath, surprised that she was actually listening to him. Had he finally gotten through to her? Maybe she'd realized when she'd seen his witness list that he wouldn't have called a guilty client to the stand. He couldn't knowingly suborn perjury. That was how his friend had nearly lost his law license—because someone had forged documents to substantiate that claim against Ronan.

But because the evidence had been forged, and proved so, the complaint had been tossed out. Now Ronan was seeing the woman who'd filed the complaint. She hadn't forged the documents, though. They had been sent to her just as the bank records had been sent to Hillary.

Who the hell was out to make trouble for Street Legal? And why?

Hillary smiled over his hesitation. "You can't come up with any other suspects, either."

"I can't come up with a name," he explained, "because no one knows what it is, but even you insist the man exists."

She sighed and settled her butt onto her desk. He wanted to lift her onto it like he had that first time he'd come to her office. He wanted to push up her skirt and push aside her panties and drive her crazy with his tongue and with his mouth.

But he drew in a deep, albeit unsteady, breath and forced himself to focus. He had made his client a promise—to do his best. And he hadn't been doing that because of her, because she distracted him, with her silky blond hair, with her full lips, with her sexy body.

Her blue eyes darkened, dilating as she stared up at him. And it was as if she could read his mind, or maybe she was reliving that first time as well.

He nearly reached for her, but he curled his fingers into his palms instead. "No."

"Yeah, it's not him," she agreed. "It's Byron."

He chuckled and shook his head. "That's not what I was denying."

"What were you denying?" she asked. And as if she knew she had him teetering on the edge, she tried his control more, reaching for the buttons of her suit coat. She flicked them open and shrugged off the jacket. It dropped onto the desk behind her.

And he swallowed hard. There was no denying his attraction to her. It was ridiculously powerful like the passion that burned between them.

He closed his eyes because he couldn't look at her—her shoulders bare but for the thin-strapped camisole she wore—and not want her. "It's the lover," he said.

"Lover?" Her voice was husky as she whispered the word. It was also close, so close that her lips brushed across his earlobe as she uttered it.

He nearly shivered in reaction to the warmth of her breath, the touch of her lips.

It wasn't fair how she affected him. Not when he was trying so hard to focus. But didn't that alone prove his point? Her point. She'd made it first.

"It was a crime of passion," he said. "Just like you said."

"So you agree?" She'd pulled back. So he opened his eyes and met her gaze. She looked almost disappointed when she should have been triumphant as she added, "You think your client's guilty, too."

He groaned with two kinds of frustration. He'd thought she was finally going to listen to him. And he wanted her. His control snapping, he reached for her, closing his hands around those sexy bare shoulders. "Damn, woman, you are so infuriating!"

She smiled and acted all innocent. "Me?"

He laughed. Nobody had ever challenged him like Hillary did. In the courtroom and out of it.

But she wasn't fighting him now. She reached for the buttons of his shirt. He'd left his jacket and tie in his SUV, along with his briefcase. Just as she had before, she jerked his shirt open. A button pinged off her desk and another off the wall.

"My dry cleaner wonders what the hell's been happening to my buttons," he teased.

"Did you tell her?" she asked.

"I showed her," he said.

She tensed and pulled back. And he saw on her face what she'd made him feel that night when he'd shown up along with dopey Dwight at her door. Jealousy.

He grinned, as something warm rushed over his heart. "What's wrong?" he asked. "Jealous?"

She narrowed her eyes in a glare. "You're just proving my point. It was a crime of passion."

"That's what I told the dry cleaner," he said.

She laughed. "You probably just threw out the shirts and bought new ones."

She knew him too damn well. That was why she was such a formidable adversary in court and such a thorough and exciting lover.

He tugged off her camisole and found another nude lace bra beneath. "Isn't that what you did?" he asked.

She shook her head. "No. I have several of these. They don't show beneath my clothes." She wrinkled her nose. "Sorry I'm not like the lingerie models and designers you date."

"Not me," he corrected her. "My partners date those women."

"What kind of women do you date?" she asked, cocking her head as if interested but also a tiny bit jealous.

He loved that jealousy on her. It felt better there than feeling it himself. "Oh, smart, practical women who buy bras that won't show beneath their clothes."

She smiled.

He fingered the strap of her bra before he reached for the clasp behind her back. He undid it and pulled it from her beautiful breasts. "But if you have more than one of these, why did you want that one back?" he asked.

Her smile turned into a grimace. "I didn't want you showing it to anyone else."

"You're the only one who saw it," he assured her.

And she released a breath of release.

"But your panties…" He waited for a long moment before adding, "…are dangling from my rear-view mirror."

And she smacked his shoulder. And laughed.

There was something about her laugh that reached inside Stone, that wrapped around his heart and squeezed it tightly. As much as he enjoyed sparring with her in court and having sex with her out of it, he enjoyed talking to her, joking around with her.

"Did I hurt you?" she asked.

It had hurt—that twinge in his heart. But he rubbed his shoulder instead and groaned. "Yeah, woman, you don't know your own strength."

"Oh, I know," she said, and she wrapped her arms around his neck and tugged his head down toward hers. Then she kissed him—deeply, passionately—her lips nibbling on his before she slid her tongue into his mouth.

She tasted like chocolate again. But it wasn't dark this time. It was smooth and mild. Milk chocolate...

He smiled against her lips. Just like the nude bra, he found it incredibly sexy. Hell, he found everything about her sexy.

That twinge struck his heart again, and he recognized it this time. It was fear.

Stone's lips stilled beneath hers. He wasn't kissing her back. He was in a strange mood tonight. Playful one minute, morose the next.

She pulled back and asked, "What's wrong?"

But he didn't answer her. He only stared at her with an intensity she'd never seen in him before. She'd always considered Stone intense. Then he lifted her up and clutched her closely to his chest. His hair tickled her nipples, making them taut and sensitive.

A moan slipped through her lips. She arched her neck, and his lips were there, sliding down her throat. He nibbled and suckled.

"Are you trying to give me a hickey for court?" she asked.

He chuckled. "That's a good idea. Maybe if you

wore a turtleneck, you wouldn't distract me so damn much."

"I distract you?"

His eyes widened as he stared. He eased her back and moved his gaze over her, from her tousled hair over her bare breasts down to her feet, which were bare too since she'd kicked off her shoes a while ago.

"You know you distract me."

She'd thought so, but she'd wondered if she'd only been fantasizing again, like she used to about him. "I thought I was just cute."

His lips curved into a grin. "I can't let you have the upper hand."

Would that always be the issue with them? They'd always be jockeying for position? For the victory?

Before she could think about it any more, he lowered his head to hers and kissed her deeply. When he pulled back, she was panting for breath, and so was he. But he managed to say, "I think you're beautiful."

It could have been a line. But that didn't seem like Stone's style. He didn't have to sweet-talk women to get them into bed, especially not her as he was already well aware. So he must have just said it because he meant it.

Warmth rushed through her heart, then moved lower, burning in her core. She wanted him so badly. Her hand shook as she reached for his belt, but she managed to unclasp it. Then she lowered his zipper and freed his penis. It was engorged, a vein standing out.

He wanted her just as badly as she wanted him. She pushed down his pants and his boxers. And her breath whistled out in appreciation. "You're the beautiful one," she murmured.

No. Stone Michaelsen didn't need to sweet-talk women to seduce them. All he had to do was be— Stone.

He shook his head, though, as if he didn't believe her. But before she could argue with him, he covered her mouth again with his. Then he covered her breasts with his hands. He cupped them and teased the nipples with his thumbs.

She moaned against his mouth. And he deepened the kiss, sliding his tongue inside, and as he did, he bunched up her skirt, pushed aside her panties and slid his fingers inside her. She was so ready for him that she nearly came then. But he pulled his hand back. As he had that first night, he lifted her onto her desk and dropped to his knees.

She would have never believed in a million years that she would bring Stone Michaelsen to his knees not once but twice. But then she was the one writhing and begging for more. She was so close…

But each time she nearly came, he pulled back and moved his tongue or his fingers.

And she murmured in frustration. "Stone…" His name was a plea.

Instead of answering, he just flicked his tongue across her clit.

"Stone!" She covered her breasts with her hands and stroked the nipples herself, and as she did, she came.

And Stone groaned. "You're going to make me come, too."

"That's the idea," she said, and she reached for him.

But he pulled back and pulled out a condom instead.

Why wouldn't he let her go down on him? Was it an issue of control?

Because he'd just had full control over her. And now he did again as he turned her over her desk so her ass was in the air. He eased his way inside her core, thrusting deep. And his hands cupped her breasts now, like she'd wanted. He stroked her nipples and nibbled on her neck as he bent over her, bent over the desk.

And he took her, thrusting deep. She arched back, grinding her butt against him—meeting his every thrust. They moved together in a frantic rhythm. He was as desperate for release as he'd just had her. She could feel it in the mad pounding of his heart against her back, in the shakiness of his hands on her breasts...

The tension wound tightly inside her again. He moved one hand from one of her breasts and stroked his thumb over her clit. And she came again, barely suppressing the urge to scream his name. But she wasn't sure they were entirely alone in the office.

Sure, it was after hours, but the cleaning crew might have been around yet. She hoped not, though, because she hadn't been quiet.

He was, as he buried his face in her neck, clutching her against him, his cock pulsating as he came. A deep groan escaped his lips.

A sound echoed it, the sound of something rattling outside the door. It must have been the cleaning crew's cart.

Hillary gasped and pulled away from him. She dressed quickly, making sure she found her bra this time.

Stone had dressed, too, but he had a gap on his shirt where two buttons were missing. "Crime of passion," he said, gesturing at the loose threads.

Hillary smiled. "You don't give up." And maybe that was it, what all having sex with her was—a way to win. Her smile slid away and she sighed before asking, "Okay, why would her lover have killed her?"

Stone's eyes brightened to a shiny silver. He thought he'd swayed her.

"I don't think you're right," she warned him. "But give me the lover's motive for killing her."

"If the husband can be jealous, so can the lover," Stone pointed out. "Maybe he wanted her all to himself, and she wouldn't leave her husband."

A little doubt began to niggle at Hillary. "You mean his millions."

"Billions," he automatically corrected her. "And yes, she knew that the prenup locked her into the marriage. If she left, she got nothing."

"But why would the lover kill her?" Hillary persisted. "Why wouldn't he kill Mueller? Then he'd get the woman and the money."

Stone groaned. "You are so damn stubborn."

She shook her head. "I'm right."

But he had a point. She needed to find out who the lover was. Then she'd know the truth beyond a reasonable doubt. And so would the jury.

"What are we?" she wondered aloud and hated herself for asking the question. Like Dwight had said, she wasn't one of those girlie girls who wanted a relationship or, worse yet, to discuss a relationship. She didn't care what they had. She knew it wasn't going to last. "Forget I asked that. I know what we are."

He arched a dark brow. "Lovers?"

"Opposing counsel," she replied.

"Really?" Stone asked. "Seems like we're both on the same page for this case. We both want justice."

She snorted. "I want justice. You want to win the trial."

"I *will* win." And he said it as if he was warning her.

Did he have some trick up his sleeve like he usually did? Was he going to use their—whatever it was—against her?

CHAPTER THIRTEEN

HE'D LIED TO HER. Stone was not convinced that he was going to win. He wasn't sure that he could, especially with his client stonewalling him.

"I can't put you on the stand," Stone said, "not until you tell me everything."

Byron stared across the conference room table at him. They weren't at the jail, which should have made it easier for Stone to relax. There was still a guard posted outside the courthouse conference room where Stone had been allowed to meet with his client before the next session began. But it wasn't the guard making him uneasy; it was the fact that he knew Byron was holding back.

"You know who her lover was," Stone said. If he knew, he must have had a reason for keeping it quiet. He certainly wasn't protecting the man with whom his young bride had been cheating on him.

Had he killed him, too? The horrible thought flickered through Stone's mind and chilled his blood.

And for once he saw what Hillary saw about his job—that he might actually be helping a killer elude justice.

And if he eluded justice, he was bound to kill again. If he hadn't already...

"She cannot be right," he murmured. About Byron or about him.

It wasn't as if Stone wanted the guilty to go free. That wasn't why he'd chosen to become a criminal defense lawyer. It was that he wanted to make sure everyone got fair representation—because his mother sure hadn't.

If only she'd been sentenced to rehab instead of jail.

She might have been able to kick her drug habit and her husband to the curb. He sighed and rubbed his hand around the back of his neck where all his tension had gathered.

This was the kind of tension that not even a soul-shattering orgasm with Hillary could ease.

Byron leaned across the table and grasped Stone's arms. "She's not right," he said. "I did not kill my wife."

"What about her lover?" Stone asked.

Byron's brow furrowed with confusion.

"Did you kill him?" he asked.

Byron's face flushed. "I am not a killer."

And once again Stone believed him. But that

didn't make his job any easier. In fact, it made it a hell of a lot harder. Just like Hillary made him.

Just thinking about her had more tension gripping him, coiling low in his groin. He groaned and shook his head. "I can't put you on the stand."

"But you believe me," Byron pointed out. "The jury will, too."

"I'm not worried about the jury," Stone said. "I'm worried about Hillary Bellows."

"What about her?"

"I think she's good," Stone said. Maybe even better than he was. "She's so good that she might be able to get out of you whatever the hell you're afraid to tell me."

Byron shook his head. "No way in hell. She won't get to me."

That was what Stone had once thought, too. He shook his head. "I can't risk it. I can't risk another damn surprise in this trial."

"So what are you going to do?"

"Ask for a recess until tomorrow," Stone said. It would buy him some time to think. If he didn't put Byron on the stand now, when the jury knew he was supposed to testify…they would think he'd changed his mind for a reason, that Byron had something to hide.

Unfortunately, they were right.

Was he? Was he only convincing himself of Byron's

innocence in order to save face with Hillary? Hell, he should be more worried about his conscience than her.

But it felt like she had become his conscience and more...

Too much more.

Hillary stood in the elevator, staring up at the numbers flashing above the doors. Her briefcase hung from her hand. It had never felt as heavy as it did right now with the envelope inside it.

Was she doing the right thing?

Should she have brought it here? Or straight to court?

Her boss had said that he wanted to be notified the minute she got any new evidence. This information would guarantee a conviction. Wilson Tremont would undoubtedly want to present it to the judge himself. He would want the win against Stone Michaelsen on his record, even though Hillary had done all the work.

She hadn't had anything to do with this, however. The evidence had just dropped into her lap like those bank statements. She didn't want to win like this.

And most especially, she didn't want to blindside Stone again.

But was it going to blindside him?

Or did he already know?

He had to know, right?

Byron Mueller was his client. Surely, he would have told Stone everything. The elevator stopped smoothly on the top floor of the building. She had no more time to think, to figure out what was the right thing to do.

The doors slid open. And Hillary wasn't sure if she was in an office or a penthouse. The floors were hardwood, the walls exposed brick, and the tall windows looked onto the lights of Midtown.

So this was how the other half lived? The half who represented the criminals and killers?

She uttered a soft sigh as she gazed around and she felt a flash of envy. She also felt a flash of empathy for the kid Stone had once been—a child of drug dealers who'd run away to live on the streets.

He'd come a hell of a long way—much farther than she had. She smiled as she thought of the different paths they'd traveled. She'd started out here with a wealthy father who'd tried to give her everything to make up for the untimely death of her young mother. She'd gone to the best boarding schools and colleges.

She'd made connections there, even more than she had through her father. But she'd wanted to make her own way, like Stone. So she'd switched to her mother's name and lived only off the meager salary she drew from the district attorney's office. And she was probably just as happy as Stone was here in the penthouse-like luxury offices of Street Legal.

Her heels clicked against the hardwood as she stepped out of the elevator. A guy met her at the glass doors of the lobby. He was stepping out of them while reaching for the security panel next to them, probably to lock them. He glanced up as he saw her.

"Ms. Bellows?"

She was usually good with faces, but she couldn't quite place his. He had dark hair and a dark complexion. And as he reached out for her hand, she noticed the tattoo peeking out beneath the cuff of his shirt-sleeve. He was a former gang member.

One who worked at the after-school program to which she'd sometimes sentenced young offenders back when she'd worked juvenile cases.

"Miguel," she greeted him. "I didn't realize you worked here." They hadn't talked about themselves, though, just about the kids they'd both been trying to save. His program was the only thing for which she'd ever asked her father for money. He still contributed—more than she did.

He nodded. "Yeah, I go way back with these guys. I haven't seen you in a while."

She felt a flash of guilt. "I haven't worked any juvenile cases in a long time."

"You're big time now, huh?"

She would be—once she won this case. And she would win. But she didn't want to win like this. "I'm not sure what big time is anymore," she admitted.

"Trying Byron Mueller," Miguel said. "That's big time."

She shrugged.

He pulled the doors open again. "You're here to see Stone."

"Is he still here?"

"Always…" His brow furrowed. "Well, it used to be that he was always the last one still in the office. But lately…"

Lately, he'd been showing up at her office. And at her apartment.

Was that why he didn't know what she knew?

Or did he know but he'd been keeping her busy so that she wouldn't find out?

Miguel held the doors for her with one beefy arm while he gestured with the other. "He's at the end of the hall toward the right. Corner office."

"Of course," she murmured. Stone Michaelsen would have a corner office.

"Since we have the whole top floor, each of the partners has a corner office or would have…"

"Would?"

"A couple of them walled up some of the windows," he said. "Guess it goes back to the streets, where you like to keep your back against the wall."

Acting impulsively, she hugged the big man. "It was great seeing you again, Miguel," she said as she pulled back. He'd reminded her that people could come a long way from where they'd started, not just materially, like Stone had, but emotionally as well.

Could Stone achieve the emotional growth that his old friend had?

Miguel smiled at her. "It's too bad you're not doing juvenile cases anymore, Ms. Bellows. You were always really fair."

That was why she was here, because it was the only fair thing to do. With new resolve, she headed down the hall toward Stone's office.

The door was open, and despite having two walls of windows, he had his back against a wall with none. It was the same wall on which the door was, so he would have seen her before she'd seen him if he was looking up.

But he had his head bowed over an open book on his desk as he rubbed the back of his neck. He already looked beaten, so he probably knew what she did.

He just didn't know that she knew, that she had the evidence in her briefcase. She didn't want to talk about that now, at least not yet. Instead, she slipped off her heels, so he wouldn't hear her coming. And she tiptoed along the wall until she came up behind him. There wasn't much space between his chair and the wall. And the minute she reached out and touched him, he pushed back the chair and nearly crushed her. Her breath escaped in a whoosh.

And he jerked forward. "Are you okay?" he asked, his gray eyes wide with concern.

"Yes," she assured him.

"What were you doing?" he asked. "Were you

going to whop me over the head with your briefcase like you did in the parking garage?"

"I didn't whop you over the head," she said. "I hit you in the shoulder."

"I'm going to be like Ernest Rapier," he said with a sigh. "So abused."

At the moment, with dark circles beneath his eyes and lines of tension around his mouth, he looked abused. Or at least exhausted. And worried.

"Yeah, like I could ever hurt you…" But even as she said it, she trailed off. She could hurt him—or at least his case—if he didn't know what she'd just learned.

He studied her face for a long moment, and as he did, a muscle twitched along his tightly clenched jaw. "I think you just might be the only one who could."

"Will this really be your first loss?" she asked.

He grinned and shook his head. "You are so damn sure of yourself."

She had even more reason to be now.

She reached out and stroked her fingers along his jaw. Stubble was already poking through his skin. But it was soft to her touch, making her fingertips tingle. "You're not," she said. "You finally realize your client is guilty?"

He groaned, and it was full of frustration. "He's not. But he's not helping me prove it."

"He's not going to testify?" she asked. He was on

the witness list, but he could still change his mind. And she could guess why he had.

"He wants to," Stone admitted. "But…"

"What?" she asked.

"You."

"What about me?"

He touched her now, gliding his fingers along the edge of her jaw. "You're too damn good."

She'd never thought he would admit it. She beamed with pride. "You know I'll get a confession out of him."

"No," he answered immediately, as if he still had no doubts about his client's innocence. But then he added, "I think you might get out of him whatever he's not willing to tell me."

And she knew. Stone had no idea what was in that envelope. Once again it had come from his office—or at least the envelope had—but he had no idea what the contents were.

"Your client isn't being forthcoming," she mused. "That can't be a first for you."

He took his hand from her face and ran it over his. And she felt a twinge of guilt. Now was not the time to needle him for his career choice. Nor was it the time—just yet—to tell him his office mole had struck again.

Instead, she pushed him back onto his chair. "Sit down and relax."

"I can't, Hillary. You know this case isn't going well."

Even better than he did. She teased him, "It is for me."

And despite his tension, his lips curled up slightly at the corners into a shadow of his usual wicked grin. "Of course you'd see it that way."

They were never going to be on the same side of a trial, which was a problem now and for the future. Because of that, there really was no future for them. But there was the moment. And in the moment, Hillary wanted to make Stone feel better. So she dropped to her knees in front of his chair.

"What are you doing?" he asked.

"Getting you to relax." But when she reached for his belt, his stomach muscles tightened and his body tensed. She trailed her fingers down his chest. "Relax…"

"Easy for you to say."

"You don't like this," she said, "giving up control."

"I haven't been in control since that first kiss," he said, "hell, even before that or I would have had the control to not kiss you in the first place."

She liked him out of control. And she proceeded to get him to lose it again. After unclasping his belt, she tugged down the tab of his zipper. Then she freed his erection from his boxers, pushing them and his pants down around his hip bones, which jutted out. He was all toned muscle and taut skin. And his penis...

It was so thick. She closed her lips over the head of it. And so long, she sucked him deep in her mouth.

And he sucked in a sharp breath. "Hillary."

She glanced up at his face, which was now flushed with passion. He leaned back in his chair, but he still wasn't relaxed. She knew what that would take.

While she couldn't relieve all the frustration he was feeling, she could relieve some of it for him.

She continued to slide her mouth up and down the length of him, sucking him deeper into her throat each time. And what she couldn't take into her mouth, she stroked with her hand, pumping it up and down.

He groaned and reached for her, his fingers tangling in her hair. But he didn't pull her away. He just held her head, fingering the strands of her hair, as she continued to bring him to the edge.

Finally, his body tensed and a deep groan tore from his throat as he threw his head back against his chair, rocking it against the wall. Then he came, filling her mouth with his sweet release.

She swallowed it down but still some trickled from the corner of her mouth. She lapped at it with her tongue. And Stone groaned again.

"You are so damn sexy and passionate and incredible," he murmured as he stared down at her with eyes that looked glazed with pleasure and awe.

She knew he wouldn't be looking at her like that

once she opened her briefcase, so she enjoyed it for a moment. But she'd known this moment was all they would have. Once she showed him what she'd received, she suspected that whatever they had or were doing would end.

CHAPTER FOURTEEN

STONE STARED DOWN at Hillary, kneeling between his legs, and a feeling more intense even than the release she'd just given him coursed through him. He was overwhelmed, awed and scared.

She scared the hell out of him. And not just because he suspected she was going to win this trial. She scared him because of how she made him feel.

Jealous.

Out of control.

And...

He wasn't sure what the hell he felt because he'd never felt it before, so he had no way of identifying it. No way of knowing what it was or how to stop it.

But he wasn't sure he wanted it to stop. He certainly didn't want to stop having sex with her. It was too good. She was too good.

He usually didn't come for blow jobs; he couldn't make himself relax or lose control enough. But with her...

Hillary had given him no choice. She'd taken his control and she'd given him pleasure unlike any he'd ever known—except in her body. He loved sliding inside her; it felt like sliding home.

He tensed as the thought brought back a rush of fear. Home had never been a good situation for him. But then, neither was this…because just like those fleeting moments his mother had been clean, this wasn't going to last, either.

He and Hillary had no future together. They would always be sitting at different tables: her for the prosecution, him for the defense.

Not that he'd presented much of a defense yet for Byron. That was what he'd been working on when she'd shown up. He'd rather focus on her than the trial, though.

He pulled her up from the floor, but he stayed sitting while she stood. He unbuttoned her jacket and pushed it from her shoulders. She wore a blouse instead of one of her camisoles—maybe because it had gotten colder, or maybe because it had a high neckline and he had left some marks on her silky skin. When he unbuttoned those buttons and pushed it off her shoulders, he saw what he'd done the other night.

"Sorry," he murmured, and he ran his fingertips over the slight discoloration.

"No, you're not," she told him.

And he grinned. "No, I'm not."

If Dwight showed up at her place for another

booty call, he'd know that she was taken now. But was she?

What the hell were he and Hillary doing? Whatever it was, he didn't want it to stop. So he reached for her bra now, unclasping it so that the nude lace dropped onto the floor with her blouse and jacket.

"Stone…" She murmured his name on a sigh.

Even before he touched them, her nipples tightened into taut peaks. He leaned forward and flicked his tongue across one while he rubbed his thumb over the other.

She moaned and trembled as if her knees were shaking. She was so damn responsive.

He reached for the button on her skirt, but his hand was shaking slightly and he fumbled as he undid it.

"You're being careful with the buttons today," she murmured.

"We've been lucky none have taken out an eye," he replied.

And she laughed that throaty laugh he loved so much. It was as sexy as her body, as her beautiful face, as her sharp mind.

She trailed her fingers over his cheekbone, beneath his eye. "You'd look sexy with a patch…" She leaned down and pressed her mouth over his, kissing him deeply. Their lips nibbled and clung to each other's, tongues teasing.

When she lifted her head, he panted. She literally took his breath away.

He unzipped her skirt and pushed it down along with the tiny bit of lace that was her panties. He had to have her, his cock hard and pulsating with need again despite the release she'd given him.

He wanted her—needed her—so badly.

She reached for his shirt and jerked it open, buttons pinging.

"You really want to see me with a patch," he murmured.

She smiled. "I really want to see your chest." But then she covered it with her hands, or as much of it as she could with her hands.

Her palms skimmed over his muscles, making his skin tingle from her touch. Then she teased his nipples, like he'd teased hers, making them pebble from the brush of her thumbs. Then she leaned down and brushed her mouth across them.

He slid his hands to her waist, gripping it as he lifted her so that she straddled his lap. He needed a condom, though, so he arched up and pulled one from his wallet.

She took it from his hand, tore it open with her teeth and rolled it over him. And he nearly came in her hand.

She was so damn sexy.

Then she arched up and guided him inside her.

And he had that feeling like he belonged—with her, inside her.

He was losing his mind as well as his control.

She began to move, rocking back and forth, bouncing up and down. The chair creaked beneath their combined weights.

Stone didn't care if it broke. He didn't care about anything but the tension winding tightly inside him. And giving her pleasure like she'd given him.

He leaned down and kissed first her lips, then her neck and her shoulders. Then he arched his back and moved his mouth lower to her breasts.

She arched back and clutched his head to her breasts as she moved, writhing on his lap. Her inner muscles tightened around him, pulling him deeper. Then her body convulsed and she cried out as she came.

He felt the heat and wetness. And his control snapped. He gripped her hips and guided her—up and down—as he thrust inside her. And finally that tension inside him broke as he came again.

He was surprised he'd had anything left. But she turned him on as no one else ever had. He leaned his forehead against hers as they both panted for breath.

"Is that why you came?" he asked.

She smiled. "I came because you're so damn good."

He smiled, too. They were so equally matched.

But that was the problem. They were too much alike. Too determined to win, even when they were on opposing sides.

"I'm glad you came," he said.

But as he said it, her smile slid away, and she dropped her gaze from his. A chill chased the perspiration from his sweat-slick skin. "You didn't come here for this," he said. Gripping her hips, he lifted her from his lap.

She shook her head and reached for her clothes. "No."

He knew he wasn't going to like the reason that she'd really come. He stood up on legs that felt suddenly wobbly. He quickly used his adjoining bathroom to clean up, and when he returned, he found her briefcase sitting open on his desk.

She stood at the windows with her back to him. She'd dressed back up in her suit. And for a moment, he felt as he did in court, like he couldn't look at her the way he looked at her when they were alone.

But they were alone now.

It didn't feel that way, though. And when he walked to his desk and looked into her open briefcase, he understood why as he stared down at the faces in the photo.

A curse slipped through his lips as he dropped back onto his chair, stunned. He should have known. If not for her—if not for being so distracted by Hillary—he might have figured it out.

She'd messed with his self-control, his head and…

No. He couldn't let her mess with his heart.

The glass of the window reflected at Hillary the room behind her back, and she saw every nuance of Stone's reaction to the photo. He hadn't known.

He reached into the briefcase and inspected the envelope lying beneath the photo. "You just got this," he said.

"Yes."

He sighed. "Of course you did or you would have already introduced it in court."

She couldn't argue that it would have been part of her prosecution.

"Why didn't you surprise me with it like you did the bank records?" he asked.

"Because now I know that you didn't send it," she said. "Now I know I'd be surprising you."

"Why don't you want to?" he asked. "It's a great tactic to catch the defense off guard."

She shrugged.

"Are you going easy on me because of what we've been doing?" he asked, and he sounded almost disappointed to think she was.

"No!" At least she hoped that wasn't the case. She couldn't lose her edge. She couldn't go all soft and sentimental over some sex.

No matter how mind-blowing that sex was.

"You know I am all about being fair," she said. "About justice."

And that was why they would never have anything beyond that mind-blowing sex.

"You'll make a great judge," he said.

"Someday," she murmured. She knew she had a lot of dues to pay and politics to play before she would achieve her goal. And she couldn't afford to be distracted the way Stone distracted her. She whirled away from the windows and walked toward his desk. "Maybe I should have saved it for court."

She reached for her briefcase but he caught her wrist. "How are you going to admit this as evidence now?" he asked. "You can't. It doesn't prove anything."

She jerked free of his grasp and stabbed at the photo. "Byron's young bride was sleeping with his son. That's why he killed her!"

He shook his head. "No. This shows who the real killer is."

She snorted. "Now you want to blame his son?"

"I told you it was her lover," he said. "I just didn't know who the lover was."

"Why can't you accept that you're representing a guilty man?" she asked.

"Because I'm not," he stubbornly insisted.

"Are you going to claim you've never represented a guilty client?" she asked.

A muscle twitched along his cheek. "No."

"Why?" she asked. "Why do you want to help the guilty elude justice?" That was something she would never be able to get over—the reason they could never really be together.

"You're a hypocrite." He called her on it. "You claim you're all about justice."

She tensed. "I am."

"Then how can you forget that everyone is entitled to a fair trial?"

His accusation rankled, making her angry, and when Hillary got angry, she argued. Hell, she argued all the time. She knew it.

"I thought maybe you became a defense lawyer because you thought your parents didn't get a fair trial," she admitted. "But then I realized that you don't represent people like your parents. You only represent rich people."

"That's not the case," he said. "I represented the guard's grandson."

"Which benefited you as much as him," she pointed out.

He ignored her. "And even if I did only represent rich people, why would that be an issue? Are you like Judge Harrison? Automatically prejudiced against the rich because you're jealous they have more than you do?"

She laughed.

"That's it, huh? You don't think rich people deserve justice, too?"

"I have nothing against rich people," she assured him. "In fact, the person I love the most in the whole world is much richer than Byron Mueller."

He tensed, and then he snorted. "Dopey Dwight? I doubt that."

"I don't love Dwight," she said.

"Who do you love?" he asked.

"My father." And with that, she swooped her briefcase off his desk, snapped it shut and stalked out of his office. It was clear that with as much as they had in common, their differences were too great to overcome.

CHAPTER FIFTEEN

STONE'S HEAD REELED with all the new information in it. Byron's kid had been sleeping with his wife. And Hillary Bellows was the daughter of one of the richest men in New York City—hell, in the world. But she didn't use his name. She used her dead mother's maiden name instead.

She hadn't told him all of that; he'd found it out on his own. Once she told him that the man she loved the most was wealthier than Mueller.

The man she loved the most...

He felt again that lurch of his stomach, as it had roiled with that emotion he hated. Jealousy.

He'd been so jealous until she'd admitted that man was her father. Then he had been confused.

But Hillary must have changed her name because she didn't want any preferential treatment. Or maybe bias.

Like the bias she was showing Byron. She refused to accept what the new evidence proved. His innocence.

Stone slapped a copy of the photo on the table in front of Byron. "You've seen this before," he said. "You hired the private investigator who took it."

After Hillary had stormed out of his office with her copy, Stone had done a little more research. He'd delved into his client's bank records again and had found the payments to the private investigator.

Byron grimaced as he glanced at it. Then he pushed it back across the table with a trembling hand. "Get it out of here!"

They were at the jail again—in the visiting room used for defendants to meet with their lawyers. Stone hated these rooms. But there was something he hated even more—when people kept stuff from him, like Hillary had kept her real identity from him and like Byron had kept the truth.

"Why didn't you tell me?" Stone asked his client.

He wanted to ask Hillary the same thing, but she'd stormed off too quickly after her revelation to give him the chance.

"It has nothing to do with anything," Byron insisted.

"Your son and wife were sleeping together," Stone said bluntly. "It has everything to do with you, especially when you're on trial for her murder."

The billionaire shook his head.

"So there's only one reason why you wouldn't have told me," Stone said.

And he should have realized it sooner. If not for Hillary distracting him, he probably would have.

"You're protecting him," Stone continued. "That's why you bought that alibi. It wasn't really for you. It was for your son. His friend claimed that both of you were with him."

Stone had been the one who'd pointed out to Byron that grand juries and regular juries discounted family members alibiing each other. That was why they'd needed his friend to swear he'd been with them both. At the time, Stone had thought the friend was telling the truth, though—until Hillary had produced those bank statements.

Just like she'd produced the photo.

Who the hell was this mole that he or she kept getting ahold of documents like this? Someone close to Stone? Someone at the office?

He didn't have time to worry about that now. He had to make sure his client didn't go to prison for something he hadn't done.

"My son doesn't need protecting," Byron said. "He didn't do anything wrong. She's the one who seduced him, who tricked him. He wouldn't have betrayed me if she hadn't manipulated him into it."

"I wasn't talking about his sleeping with her," Stone said. He didn't care about that. Adultery was Ronan's concern, not his. Ronan was the divorce lawyer. Stone was the one who represented criminals. That was what Hillary thought. But even she would have to eventually admit that his client was innocent. "He killed your wife."

Byron tensed. And Stone knew it was the truth. He saw the pain all over his client's face, the guilt and regret and horror. He suspected Byron might have even been an eyewitness to the murder.

"We need to talk to the ADA," he said.

Now she would have to accept that he was right. His client was innocent.

And he wasn't sure why it was so important that she knew. Was it so that she would drop the charges against Byron? Or was it so she would see Stone wasn't the bad guy she'd thought he was?

He cared about justice as much as she did. Maybe more. Because he didn't just want to win; he wanted to make sure the right person paid for the crime.

Stone must have shown the photo to his client and let him know that she had it, too.

Byron Mueller knew it was all over now. He was certain to be convicted once she submitted the evidence. What did he want? Murder two?

That was the conviction she was certain to get with no negotiating with him and his high-priced lawyer. And knowing Stone, he probably wanted something less.

Manslaughter.

She snorted. That wasn't going to happen. No matter how good he was in bed.

This wasn't about sex. This was about justice.

Bethany deserved it. She'd died way too young.

The jail guard stepped back and opened the door for Hillary. With a nod of appreciation, she stepped over the threshold into the small visitation room. She visited the jail a lot. But given his clientele, Stone did as well.

Did it bother him when he did? Did it remind him of visiting his parents? Or hadn't he ever visited them? Since he'd run away from them, maybe not.

Unlike his client, who was seated at a table, Stone was standing and pacing the small confines of the room like a feral cat who'd been caged. And she knew this wasn't where he wanted to be, which was probably how he'd felt as a kid.

She felt a twinge of regret over his childhood. It had sucked. But instead of turning to a life of crime, he'd...

Chosen to help criminals.

Really, what was the difference?

She couldn't see it. And because she couldn't see it, she couldn't see a future for them. Not that she wanted a future with him—or with anyone else. Hell, nobody knew whether or not they had a future.

Her mother had found that out, way too young.

She drew her attention from Stone, took the chair across from Byron Mueller and focused on him. He didn't look like the brash billionaire who was used to either buying or bullying to get whatever he wanted. But maybe he'd realized that he couldn't buy his freedom.

"So why did you want to see me?" she asked, but she directed the question at Byron—not his attorney. She didn't want to talk to Stone after the way they'd left things, after he'd accused her of being unfair.

He didn't know her at all. Even Miguel had said she was fair.

"No offense, Ms. Bellows," Mueller said. "But I didn't want to see you."

She had to glance at Stone now. He'd stopped pacing to stand beside Byron's chair. "So why am I here? I thought your client had an admission to make."

"You know what the admission is," Stone said. "That his wife was having an affair with his son."

"Yes…" She furrowed her brow with confusion. "I am well aware of that, and I know your client is, too. The private investigator he hired is the one who took that photograph." The PI hadn't sent it to her, though, and he claimed he didn't know how it had gotten out. His client—Mueller—had told him to destroy it.

She figured someone had hacked his computer. He'd taken the photo with a digital camera and downloaded it. He probably hadn't deleted it from everything.

Mueller glanced nervously at his lawyer. He must have been surprised she knew so much.

Stone didn't look surprised. He would have known that she would do her research before submitting the photo as evidence in court.

"The private investigator is going to testify that you came unglued when he showed you that photo," she continued.

Mueller's face flushed.

"You'll have to get it admitted as evidence first," Stone said.

"I will."

"You already rested your case," he reminded her.

She chuckled. "But I can submit that photo as a rebuttal to your client's claim that he didn't know his wife was having an affair."

"My client hasn't testified on his own behalf," Stone said. "And he won't have to now."

"No, he won't have to testify," she agreed. "But he will have to give up the details of his crime in his allocution when he accepts the plea I offer him."

Stone snorted now. "Fuck your plea. He hasn't committed any crime, and you know it. How can you not drop the charges?"

"How can you be so delusional?" she demanded. But then, she'd been delusional like that when she used to fantasize about him. Sure, some of those things had happened. They'd had sex. But they had no future. "That photo goes to your client's motive. He's guilty!"

"Tell her," Stone prodded Mueller, nudging one of the older man's stooped shoulders. The guy looked like he'd aged a lot in jail and that he hadn't been eating well, if at all. The orange jumpsuit hung on a frame that had once been pudgy. "Tell her that your son did it."

She let her mouth drop open in shock as she looked from the attorney to the client. She addressed Stone first. "I knew you were desperate to win this case. But you're going to make the man throw his own son under the bus?"

Then she turned toward Mueller. "And you're going to do it? You're going to point the finger of blame at your own son? What? Out of revenge?"

"You're wrong," Mueller said, "about me. I'm not going to blame my son. You're right about my lawyer. He will do anything to win. He now has a two-million-dollar bonus riding on the jury deciding I'm not guilty."

She sucked in a breath.

And Mueller added, "He would do anything to win this trial."

Even her? Was that the only reason he'd had sex with her? He'd hoped to distract her enough that she would lose the case. Or had he hoped she would fall in love with him and just drop the charges like he'd requested?

Yes, she was right. Stone didn't know her at all. And he never would.

CHAPTER SIXTEEN

ANGER COURSED THROUGH Stone, and he didn't know who he was angrier at: his client for refusing to speak the truth or Hillary for refusing to listen. Even if Byron had talked, Stone doubted she would have believed anything he said about the murder.

The only thing she had listened to and believed was the two-million-dollar bonus Stone would receive for a not-guilty verdict. That that was the only reason Stone was so determined to win.

The minute Byron had told her that, she'd jumped up from the chair and pounded on the door for the guard to let her out. Before she'd stepped out, she'd turned back to him—and the look she'd given him.

Stone shivered at the iciness of her blue eyes. He hadn't thought she—with all her passion—could ever look that cold. Did she think the only reason he'd kissed her and had had sex with her was to get that not-guilty verdict?

Damn it!

And damn Byron Mueller for not telling the truth. He'd refused to talk to Stone, too, and had had the guard bring him back to his cell. Apparently, he'd rather rot behind bars than implicate his son.

Stone could understand wanting to protect your kid. But when that kid was a killer...

He shivered, but maybe it was just because the November wind whipped through his clothes as he hurried down the street from the Tombs. Hillary must have gone down into the subway, because he didn't catch a glimpse of her. So he hurried to his car and drove straight to her apartment.

He suspected she'd gone there instead of her office. But when he rang her bell, he could detect no movement inside. He heard something behind him, a soft gasp as she turned the corner from the elevators and saw him.

With his driving, he'd beaten her home. Of course, it looked, from the bag that she was carrying, like she'd stopped to pick up dinner.

"Candy bars?" he asked her, his pulse quickening as he remembered how the chocolate tasted on her lips, in her mouth.

"What are you doing here?" she asked. "Harassing me?"

The wind and the drive had cooled his anger—until now. Now it whipped through him even more sharply than the wind. But instead of chilling him, it made him hot. "Did I ever do anything that you didn't want me…" He stepped closer and, lowering his head and his voice, whispered in her ear, "…to do to you…"

She shivered. "I'm not upset about *what* you— we—did," she said.

He was glad that she'd owned her part in their after-hours adventures.

"I'm upset about *why* you did it."

"I had no reason," he said. No ulterior motives. He hadn't had a thought in his head except desire that first time he'd kissed her.

"You had two million reasons why," she said.

"It was only one until recently," he said.

She swung her hand toward his face. He would have let it connect if he'd had it coming. But he'd done nothing wrong. So he caught her wrist and jerked her against him.

Her eyes widened; he hoped it wasn't out of fear for how he'd reacted but because she felt his reaction to her closeness. Because even as furious as he was with her, he still wanted her.

He always wanted her.

He rubbed his erection against her belly. "This is why," he said. "Because I want you."

"You want me to drop the charges against your client," she said. And instead of melting into him, like she usually did, her body was stiff and tense.

"Yes, I do," he admitted. "But I'm not using sex to manipulate you into doing that."

"Then why after years of never noticing me did you suddenly kiss me?" she asked. And she was the one backing him up against the wall now, like she sometimes got in the face of a hostile witness to get them to crack.

Stone just grinned. "Why the hell do you think I never noticed you? I've lusted after you for years, Hillary Bellows. I just had self-control until we were finally alone together." That had been his downfall.

She was his downfall.

Her blue eyes narrowed and she studied him through her lashes.

So he turned the tables on her. "What about you? Why are you having sex with me?" he asked. "Was it just so you could distract me so much with thoughts of being with you, of being inside you?" He groaned as he thought of it, of how damn wonderful it felt moving inside her.

And a little moan slipped through her lips. She'd been holding her keys in her hand, along with her bag of food; they jingled as she turned toward her door with them and suddenly jammed them into the lock.

He knew she wanted to feel it, too—what he felt every time they were together. The passion. The heat.

The rightness.

"If that was your plan," he said, as he lowered his head to brush his lips across the nape of her neck, "it worked. You've distracted the hell out of me!"

The locks clicked, and she pushed open the door.

He waited—uncertain what to expect. Had he gotten through to her? Or was she still as icily furious as she'd been at the Tombs?

When she turned back toward him, her eyes weren't cold. They were dark, dilated with desire. She reached out, but instead of slapping him, like she had earlier, she grabbed his tie and tugged him into the apartment with her.

The door slammed behind Stone. He wasn't certain if she'd kicked it or he had. He covered her hand on his tie and asked, "Are you going to use this to strangle me?"

"I should," she told him.

"Why?" he asked.

"You know why. You never told me about that bon—"

He covered her lips with his fingers. "No. Why did you kiss me back that first time I kissed you?"

Her face flushed, and her eyes got bright. She sighed and admitted, "Because I lusted after you for years."

He couldn't help the grin from spreading across his face. "Really?"

"Like you didn't know," she said.

He shook his head. "I had no clue."

She tugged his tie free and let it drop to the floor. Then she moved on to the buttons of his shirt. She didn't rip them open this time. Instead, she took her time with each one, slowly opening his shirt. "How can you look like this and not know every woman in court is lusting after you?"

He chuckled. "I thought you hated me," he said.

"I do," she readily replied.

Even as a pang struck his heart, he laughed again. "Really?"

"Of course. You represent rich and privileged clients."

"You're rich and privileged," he reminded her.

She wrinkled her nose at him. "No. My father is."

And she'd made certain not to trade in on that. He respected that. If only she respected him, too.

"I don't hate you," he told her.

She tilted her head and studied his face. "But you hate losing."

He couldn't deny that. "I do."

"And you'd do anything to win," she said, repeating his client's words.

"That's not why I kissed you."

"Word got out around the Meet Market that you and your partners deliberately set out to seduce women to get what you want."

He pulled back and stared down at her, dumbfounded. "I don't know what surprises me more—that you go to the Meet Market, or that you'd listen to gossip about us."

"Gossip?" she said. "That's all it is?"

Damn, she was too good.

"Simon and Ronan might have done something

like that," he admitted. "But they were just trying
to find the office mole."

"That's why you came to see me that first night,"
she said. "You wanted to find out how I got that information about Mueller's alibi. Did you think I was
the office mole?"

"You don't have access to our office," he said.

She smiled. "Miguel and I go way back."

"Are you the office mole?" he asked.

She arched a brow. "Guess you'll have to seduce
me to find out."

He laughed again. He'd been so angry with her
just a short time ago. What was it about her that be-
guiled him so much that he forgot the anger—that
he forgot everything but how much he wanted her?

What the hell was wrong with her?

Hillary never should have allowed him into her
apartment. Hell, she hadn't allowed him inside; she'd
dragged him through the door with her. And just like
that day he'd kissed her in her office, she was the one
who'd undressed him.

His shirt hung open over his chest, glimpses of
muscles dusted with dark hair teasing her. Maybe
that was why she'd lost her mind. Why she was flirting with him.

The sight of his body turned her mind to mush.

It had to be mush for her to want him as much as
she did. It was almost as if she needed him.

But that wasn't possible. Hillary had never needed anyone. She'd gotten along just fine after her mother had died. And leaving her father for boarding school hadn't bothered her a bit. She'd made friends wherever she'd gone. And if they left her for other schools, she'd made more. But she hadn't needed them, either.

She'd never needed anyone. So, of course, she didn't need Stone. But she did want him—badly— at the moment.

"I am not like my partners," he told her. "I am not a charmer. I just say it like it is. So no, I cannot seduce anyone."

He had no idea.

"You don't need charm for seduction," she told him.

"I don't?"

She rose on her tiptoes and skimmed her lips along his jaw, down his neck. His pulse leaped beneath her mouth. "All you need is your lips." She pressed hers to his. But she kept the kiss brief, pulling back. Then she skimmed her fingertips down his chest. "And your touch."

"Ohhhh…" he said, and he smacked his forehead as if he'd had a sudden realization. "You're right. I did seduce you."

"Yes, you did," she said and was surprised that a giggle slipped out.

"Or did you seduce me?"

"I don't know." And she didn't care anymore. Because he was kissing her, sliding his lips across hers to her ear and her neck.

She shivered in reaction as her skin tingled. Then he touched her, skimming his hands down her sides to her hips, then over her ass. He found the button on her skirt, undid it and her zipper, and the skirt fell down. Then he pushed off her jacket, which she'd already unbuttoned in the elevator. She wore a thin sweater beneath it. He lifted that over her head and tossed it onto the floor, too.

She stood before him in just her bra and underwear. But it was her new bra and underwear. She'd splurged on some sexy lingerie she'd been seeing advertised everywhere.

And she was glad that she had when she saw his reaction. His whole body tensed and his breath escaped in a whoosh like he'd been kicked—hard.

"Damn, woman!" he exclaimed. "What the hell do you have on?"

She touched one of the cups of the bra, which was secured to the strap with a bow. "Bette's Beguiling Bows."

He shook his head. "No damn wonder Simon lost his mind…and Ronan."

"What?" she asked, totally confused what his partners had to do with her new underthings.

"The lingerie designer, the model…" He gestured at her underwear. "That's what they do."

And his partners did them, apparently.

"Shouldn't I have bought it?" she asked.

"Depends," he said and he pushed her fingers away from the bow to toy with it himself. He tugged it loose so that the cup dropped away, freeing her breast. He cupped it in his palm and flicked his thumb across the nipple.

And she lost her breath for a moment as pleasure streaked from her breast to her core. "On what?"

He moved his hand from her breast to the bow holding up the other cup. He toyed with the end of the bow for a long moment before pulling it loose. Then he cupped that breast in his hand, but he held his thumb just a breath away from the nipple.

"On what?" she asked, as desire burned inside her.

"Did you buy it for me or dopey Dwight?"

She smiled. "You."

And he touched her nipple, rubbing his thumb across it. Once. Twice. "But you were mad at me and I was mad at you."

"We usually are," she said.

He nodded. "That's right. You hate me."

"I do." But her heart felt all warm and big, and she was afraid that she didn't hate him enough. She needed to hate him more. "That was another reason I bought this," she said. "Figured I would let you sneak a peek and then deny you."

"There's one problem with that," he said, and he pulled that hand away and stepped back.

"What's that?" she asked, and her brow furrowed.

"If you deny me, you deny yourself, too." And he turned as if he was going out the door.

She cursed. Him and herself.

But he only turned the dead bolt before whirling back toward her and lifting her in his arms. He headed straight toward the bedroom.

They denied each other nothing. Their mouths and hands moved hungrily over each other. He tugged loose the bows on her hips that had held her panties together. Then he slid his fingers inside her. He teased her, intensifying the pressure inside her, the need for release until she squirmed on the mattress.

She held out her arms, trying to pull him down with her. She had never needed anyone before, but in this moment—in the heat of passion—she needed him.

Finally, he stepped back and pushed down his pants and boxers. Then he sheathed himself before joining her on the bed. He lifted her legs, hooking them around his shoulders as he eased himself inside her.

She had never considered herself a flexible person until now. She was able to bend and contort so that he slid even deeper inside her.

The sensation was incredible. He was incredible.

He leaned over more and kissed her—deeply, hungrily—as he set a frantic rhythm. She joined him, grinding her hips against him, meeting his every thrust, until finally that unbearable tension broke.

He slipped away for a few moments before coming back and crawling into bed. He rolled her limp, satiated body into his arms and held her closely.

She had never been so satisfied. So content. So happy...

But then she tensed as she realized she was falling for him. She was beginning to need him. That could not happen.

"What's wrong?" he asked as he stroked her back.

But his voice sounded funny, almost strangled as if emotions were getting to him, too.

"We have to stop doing this," she said.

"You dared me to seduce you," he reminded her.

She knew. And it had been stupid. "You know this will never work."

"This?" he asked. "What is this?"

"Wrong," she said. "We're on opposite sides of this trial."

"A trial that shouldn't even be happening," he said. "You need to drop the charges."

She rolled out of bed and picked up his clothes from the floor, throwing them at him. "That is the only reason you've been kissing me, having sex with me—you want me to help you get that two million dollars."

"Hill—"

"It's all about money with you!" she accused him.

"That's why you represent the clients you represent. You don't care that you could be putting a killer out on the streets—"

"And you don't care that an innocent man could go to prison," he said. "It's better that ten guilty men go free than one innocent man suffer."

"Don't throw that quote at me," she said. "You know you've helped more than ten guilty men go free."

"So you're going to make Byron Mueller pay for that?" he asked.

"No. I'm going to make Byron Mueller pay for killing his wife."

Stone just shook his head as he pulled on his clothes. "It's like you're determined to think the worst of me for some reason," he said.

"I didn't say you murdered your wife," she said.

"But you won't believe anything I tell you."

"I can't trust you."

"Why not?" he asked.

She grabbed the tangled sheet from the bed and wrapped it around herself. She didn't want to have this conversation naked. She didn't want to have this conversation at all. "You know why."

"Because I'm a defense lawyer?" he asked. "C'mon, Hillary, you know everyone's entitled to a fair trial. Is it just me or can't you trust anyone?"

Maybe that was the problem. But she wasn't about to admit that to him.

"Is it because your mom died when you were so young? Then your dad shipped you off to boarding schools. Don't you trust people to stick around?"

She gasped with shock. "You've done your research on me," she said. "Or did you have Allison McCann pull up that dirt for a press release? Going to use that against me?"

"Hill—" He reached out for her, but she slapped his hand away.

"Get out of here," she said. "I'll see you in court tomorrow unless you have the sense to accept a plea for your client. Murder two."

He shook his head. "I'm not going to plead for an innocent man." And she suspected he wasn't talking just about Byron now. He was talking about himself. He didn't think he'd done anything wrong.

But he'd done everything wrong.

He'd made her fall in love with him.

But she'd get over it—just like she had everything else in her life. She lifted her chin and shored up her resolve. "Fine. It'll be better to beat you in court, anyway."

"That's all you really care about," he said. "Winning. Not justice." He headed out of her room, and seconds later, the apartment door slammed.

She would win. And yet she knew the victory would feel hollow, not because she had any doubts about Mueller's guilt—but because she'd lost Stone.

CHAPTER SEVENTEEN

"ALL OF THE evidence presented in this courtroom has proved what I told you that very first day," Hillary said as she stood before the jury. Then she turned back and pointed toward the defense table. "This man is a bad man."

And like the first time she'd said it, Stone wasn't sure if she was referring to him or his client.

"He thinks he is above the law," she said. "He paid a man to lie and alibi him."

And now she pointed her finger directly at Stone. "He offered his lawyer a two-million-dollar bonus for getting a not-guilty verdict."

Stone flinched. And Byron clutched his arm. "Can't you object?"

"You told her," Stone murmured. But he should have told her more: the truth.

She turned back to the jury. "I hope you send him the message that your integrity cannot be bought. That nobody is above the law."

Stone stood to offer his argument. But he had no rabbit to draw out of a hat—nothing like his usual flash and pomp. His client had tied his hands. He did his best.

But it wasn't enough. He saw it in the disapproving faces of the jury. They thought, like Hillary, that he was just all about the money.

Two million dollars. He didn't care about the money at all. He cared that Byron Mueller was going to die in prison for a crime he hadn't committed.

But there was nothing more he could do. To save Byron or himself.

Hillary had shut him out—and not just out of her apartment the other night. She'd shut him out of her life. Maybe he'd crossed a line, but he'd only been trying to get through to her.

But she was too closed off. She'd found a way to protect herself, just like he had all these years. But at least he'd let his friends get close to him. He suspected she'd let no one close.

She didn't want to need anyone.

He wasn't too proud to admit he needed his friends—hours later—after the verdict had been returned. Simon patted his back where he sat, slouched at the bar to which they'd dragged him. "It's too bad, man…"

He wasn't sure if Simon was commiserating because he'd lost the case or the two-million-dollar bonus. But unlike Hillary, he was willing to give his friend the benefit of the doubt. She hadn't given that to him or his client.

And neither had the jury.

"How could they not have reasonable doubt?" he asked.

"She presented a strong case," Trev said, but he'd dropped his voice to a low whisper, as if he didn't want to be overheard admitting it. "Maybe you should have had Allison go after her harder in the press."

He could have. He could have gone after her in his closing argument, too. He could have said she was biased against his client because he was a rich billionaire like the father who'd abandoned her after her mother died. But Hillary wasn't on trial.

And he couldn't have hurt her like that.

Like she'd hurt him.

Of course, she hadn't said anything that wasn't true. His client had offered him a hefty bonus. A bribe?

"Do you think," Trev continued, "that he could be guilty?"

Stone shook his head. But she'd obviously swayed his partner. "No, it was his kid who killed her. I'm sure of it."

"Or do you just want that to be the case, because you'd convinced yourself you were representing the good guy?" Ronan asked. That was how, as a divorce lawyer, he broke down his cases. There was a good guy and a bad guy. And he always thought he was representing the good guy. But he'd been fooled recently and had wound up hurting the good guy—or in this case, beautiful woman.

Muriel had forgiven him, though.

He wasn't sure that Hillary would. But he hadn't done anything wrong. She was the one who'd sent an innocent man to prison.

Stone shook his head again. "No. I'm sure the kid did it. Byron all but admitted it to me. But he wouldn't give a statement to Hillary."

"He's protecting his kid?" Simon said as if shocked at the prospect. And given how his con artist father had set him up to take the rap for their earlier cons, it was no wonder he would be shocked.

Stone was, too. His father had set up his mother to take the fall for some of his drug deals. Not that she hadn't been complicit as well. He had no doubt that eventually his father would have had him selling drugs, too, if he hadn't run away.

"You said the kid was the one cheating with the wife," Ronan said and shook his head. "Can't believe he'd protect him after that."

If his own partners didn't believe him, it was no wonder that Hillary hadn't. Maybe he had been too hard on her.

And he realized that the sick hollow feeling in his stomach wasn't just because he'd lost the case. It was because he'd lost Hillary.

* * *

Despite her victory, Hillary had that sick hollow feeling in her stomach that she'd feared she would have. She'd won the case, but she'd lost Stone. He'd seemed more devastated over the verdict than Byron Mueller had.

The press, of course, was having a field day with that. Stone's handsome face was all over the news, the headlines reading Street Legal criminal attorney devastated to lose…two-million-dollar bonus.

That had been a low blow, even for her. She shouldn't have included that. She closed out of the news browser on her computer. The office was quiet. Everyone else must have gone home. Nobody had offered to take her out for a drink to celebrate—maybe because her boss was furious she'd won. He'd wanted the victory for himself. And of course, it hadn't helped that the press reports had said she was certain to get his job now.

She didn't want his job, though. She wasn't even certain she wanted the judgeship now. Stone might have been right that she was already too judgmental.

Not that she was, though.

Byron Mueller had to be guilty. A jury of his peers had convicted him. She'd had all the evidence.

But why did she suddenly feel as if she'd missed something? Then she realized what she missed:

Stone.

He was the person with whom she wanted to celebrate her victory. But that wasn't possible when they were always on opposite sides. She was smart to have ended this thing—whatever it was—with him.

Sure, she'd fallen for him. But she'd get over it. Just like she'd gotten over the death of her mother and not seeing much of her father.

She stared at the cell phone she'd left sitting on her desk. A few law school friends had texted congratulations to her. Dwight hadn't. She didn't know if he was mad about the Stone thing or if he'd taken her advice and was trying complicated.

Would it work for him? It might. He didn't have the history Hillary did. She knew it wouldn't work for her. No. It was better that it had ended now with Stone before she'd gotten attached or something.

Not that she'd ever really been attached to anyone or anything.

But when knuckles rapped on her door, her heart jumped and warmed with hope. Was it Stone?

"Come in!" she called out, and she winced at the eagerness in her voice.

Maybe he hadn't been as upset about losing as he'd looked. Maybe he'd realized that she was right, that his client was guilty.

When the door slowly opened, it wasn't Stone standing there. She immediately recognized the young man from the photo the private investigator had taken and from court. He hadn't taken the stand in his father's defense. While his friend had testified

that the two of them had been with him at the time
of the murder, the kid hadn't corroborated that testi-
mony. She'd thought at the time that it was because
the friend had perjured himself for the big payout
Byron Mueller had given him.

Now she had a niggling feeling in her stomach
that made her feel even sicker than she'd already
been feeling.

It wasn't unusual for a defendant's family to seek
her out after a verdict and request leniency. Or for
her to somehow revert the verdict. Maybe that was
why Kenneth Mueller was here. Maybe Stone had
even sent him.

But usually he was more direct than that. Since
she was, too, she asked, "Why are you here, Mr.
Mueller?"

"Why are you?" he asked, and there was bellig-
erence in his voice that made her nervous. She had
a panic button under her desk, one that would alert
security if she thought she was in danger.

Why hadn't she used it that first night that Stone
had come to her office? It would have saved her a
lot of heartache. Because her heart was aching now.

"I thought you'd be out celebrating your big victory over billionaires and Stone Michaelsen," he
sniped at her as he dropped onto one of the chairs
in front of her desk.

"Looks like you've been celebrating enough for

both of us," she mused as she noted his red eyes. Had he been drinking or using?

She'd known so many kids in boarding school who had turned to drugs and alcohol, like those substances could replace the love and attention their busy parents denied them.

He rubbed at his eyes, and she realized he hadn't been partying. He'd been crying. He shook his head, as if too choked up to speak.

"Guess you have billions of reasons to celebrate," she mused, but she was just pushing now—to see how he would react. How long would it take security to get up here if she had to push the panic button? She was more concerned with getting the truth than she was with her safety, though. So she continued, "With your father in prison, all of his money will be yours now."

"No!" he shouted. "I told her I wouldn't do it. And I won't do it now."

"What?" she asked.

"I won't kill my father."

New York State didn't have the death penalty. But she refrained from pointing that out to young Mueller.

"Who asked you to kill your father?"

"Bethany," he said. "That's the only reason she was sleeping with me. She was trying to turn me against my dad." He sniffled. And she realized that even though he was twentysomething, maturity-wise he was much younger. Bethany must have realized, and exploited, that lack of maturity.

"She got that gun out," he said. "She'd stolen the keys from him somehow. But she was careful to use gloves. She made me put on some, too, before she handed the gun to me. She wanted me to use it to kill my dad, to make it look like a suicide."

"Suicide?"

"Because he knew about us, people would think he was so devastated that he took his own life," Kenneth explained. "But that wasn't the truth. He was going to throw her out on the street. So she wanted me to kill him. She said that it was the only way we could be together and have all his money."

He sniffled again. "That was all she wanted. The money. Not my dad. Not me…" His voice cracked with sobs. "And she thought that I would do it…that I would kill him. And instead I turned the gun on her, and I just pulled the trigger…" He stared down at his hand as if he could see the gun in it yet, and he looked as shocked as he must have been then.

He shuddered.

And Hillary found herself shuddering in sympathy. She couldn't imagine what it must have felt like for him to take a life. But she felt as if she had nearly taken one herself for getting that guilty verdict for an innocent man. With the sentence he was bound to have received, Byron Mueller would have died in prison.

"I didn't know I was going to do it," Kenneth murmured. "But she kept pushing and pushing for me to do it. And, in that moment, it felt like it was her or my dad."

She found herself reaching across her desk to pat the back of his shaking hand.

He looked up at her again and tears overflowed his eyes. "I—I couldn't kill my dad," he said. "He's been so good to me—my whole life. He's given me everything I ever wanted. And he even helped out all my friends..." His voice cracked again. "He's such a good guy...and I already betrayed him with *her*."

He turned his hand over and clasped hers, squeezing. "Please, don't let him do this for me. Don't let him go to prison for something I did."

"Why didn't you come forward earlier?" she asked.

"Because he was sure his lawyer could get him off."

That was why he'd offered Stone the two-million-dollar bonus. Not for himself but for his son.

Byron Mueller's only crime was being a doting father. Regret squeezed her heart even more tightly than Kenneth was squeezing her hand.

"But Stone Michaelsen wasn't as good as my dad thought he was," Kenneth bitterly remarked. "He couldn't even get an innocent man off."

"Your father wouldn't help him," she said. "He

refused to tell Stone everything." But he'd figured it out anyway. He'd been right the whole time.

"Is it too late?" Kenneth asked. "Is there any way for me to fix this—to finally take responsibility?"

"You just did," she assured him. "We'll figure this out. First, you need to get a lawyer. And I'll book you on the charge of voluntary manslaughter." She already knew that if Stone was representing him, that was the charge he'd get for his client. And given the circumstances, it was probably the right one.

"Can you call Stone Michaelsen?" he asked. "That's who my father will have represent me. And when can we get my dad out of jail?"

"You'll have to allocute to the crime," she said, "and the judge will have to accept your plea before your father will be released."

"He can't get out now?" he asked, and he sounded like a child again. His father had probably never made him wait for anything, so he had no idea how due process worked. Or how life worked…

She understood why his father had chosen to go to prison for him. Kenneth Mueller wouldn't make it there. He wasn't mature or strong enough.

And his father loved him.

"He'll be fine."

But instead of reassuring him, her words had him sobbing harder again. She needed to book the kid. She glanced at the time on her phone. It was probably too late to get him in front of a judge for a bail hearing, anyway. He would have to spend the night at the Tombs. But he needed to have his lawyer present to officially take down the statement he'd just given her.

She reached for her cell phone and pressed in the contact for Stone. But it wasn't his deep voice that answered her call. She couldn't be sure who it was, though, for all the background noise. But she suspected it was one of his partners.

"I need to speak to Stone," she said.

"What? You want to gloat?" the man asked her. "You going to rub your victory in his face?"

"No. But I need to see him," she said.

The man snorted derisively. "Well, he's a little busy right now. We're all at the Meet Market."

And she heard the tinkle of a woman's laugh in the background. And Stone's deep voice murmuring something in reply. And her heart broke.

She felt like laying her head on her arms and crying like Kenneth Mueller was. But she was stronger and more mature than that. She'd had to be.

"Well, when he's done partying, tell him Kenneth Mueller is in my office confessing to the murder for which his father was just convicted."

"What?"

"Tell Stone he was right," she said, even though the words panged her nearly as much as hearing him making another woman laugh, like he'd always made her laugh.

"Hillary, wait—"

She said nothing more, just clicked off that call to make another. To the detective who'd handled—or actually mishandled—the homicide investigation. Unlike Stone, he was going to come right to her office.

Stone was busy—hooking up with another female. He hadn't really wanted her at all.

He'd just wanted to win.

Well, he had his win now.

She hoped it felt as hollow for him as it had for her.

CHAPTER EIGHTEEN

STONE HAD A killer headache and a killer client. He'd had too much to drink the night before. Muriel and Bette had joined him and the guys at the bar. They'd felt sorry for him, not because of his loss in court but because of his loss in love. So they'd bought him a few rounds of shots.

Usually Stone could handle his liquor. But he hadn't had anything to eat that day or probably the day before. He was too sick over the trial, but mostly over Hillary.

It wasn't love, though. He'd scoffed at the idea of that, but everyone around him—even Trev—had exchanged knowing looks, like they'd all thought he was kidding himself.

Sure, Hillary excited him more than any other woman ever had. She made him better in court and in bed. She challenged him as no one ever had. She matched him.

If only she could love him.

But she didn't respect him. And they couldn't build a relationship if they didn't have mutual respect. He respected her. According to Trev, who had answered his phone the night before, she'd admitted she was wrong—about Byron.

What about him?

He stared across the desk at her, and he couldn't help but think of the things that they'd done on that desk.

The things he wanted to do to her even now. Suddenly his tie felt too tight and so did his pants. How could she get to him so effortlessly?

Maybe Kenneth Mueller shouldn't have asked for him to represent him. He'd failed his father because of Hillary—because she'd distracted him so much that he hadn't been able to exonerate an innocent man.

Until now...

But Kenneth had done that when he'd gone to Hillary with his confession the night before. Since Stone hadn't been available, the kid had waived his right to have a lawyer and had written down his statement anyway.

But Stone could get that tossed out—if he wanted to. Since Kenneth had let his dad spend months in jail already for his crime, he wasn't sure he even wanted to represent the kid at all, though.

"Do you need some coffee, Mr. Michaelsen?" she

asked. "You probably need some caffeine to wake up after your late night at the bar."

All he needed was her. The thought stunned him. But it was true. He needed her. He'd never been as happy as he had been these past couple of weeks. While the trial had been nearly debilitating in its intensity, the passion and humor with her had balanced out all that—had made him feel things he'd never felt before.

Love.

Damn it, Bette and Muriel had been right. He was in love with the opposing counsel.

"Are you okay, man?" Kenneth whispered at him.

Stone nodded. "Yes." He focused on the young man; it was safer than looking at Hillary.

Even with dark circles beneath her blue eyes, she was so damn beautiful. Kenneth's eyes were red and puffy as if he'd spent the entire night crying.

Hillary obviously hadn't. But then, like dopey Dwight had said, she wasn't the girlie kind, so it wasn't like she'd spent the night eating ice cream and weeping over a lost love. Well, first she would have had to love him to do that. And she wouldn't have pushed him away like she had if she'd had any deep feelings for him.

He forced himself to turn back toward her and ask, "What are you offering?" He wanted her heart, but he knew she wasn't going to offer him that. Hell, she wasn't going to offer him anything.

Only his new client.

"Voluntary manslaughter, first degree, minimum sentence at a minimum-security prison."

He let a gasp slip out.

"What?" Kenneth asked. "Is that bad?"

Stone shook his head. "It's fair." Hell, it was more than fair.

"You're—you're not going to negotiate?" Kenneth asked.

He shook his head. "The faster you agree and allocute, the faster your father will get out. And it is a good deal." He swallowed his pride and admitted, "A very good deal."

Kenneth nodded and turned back toward her. "Thank you, Ms. Bellows. Thank you!"

She offered him a smile, even though she'd denied Stone one. "We'll get your father out as soon as we can."

"Thank you!" Kenneth said again. He looked like an excited puppy about to piss all over himself he was so eager to please her.

Stone knew the feeling. He wanted to please Hillary, too. He wanted to drive her out of her mind with pleasure, like she'd always driven him.

But even more important than that, he just wanted to be with her—to tease her and laugh with her. And hold her...

God, he was the girlie one.

He rose from his chair when Kenneth stood. The

judge had agreed to release him on bond as long as he wore a tether. It was strapped to his ankle. The kid glanced down at it. "Can I just leave?" he asked.

"You have to go straight home," Stone reminded him.

"Can I go see my father first?"

Hillary nodded. "I'll make a call and let the monitoring company know."

Kenneth showered his gratitude on her again before leaving her office. She'd already picked up the phone to call the monitoring company when Stone started to head out. She obviously didn't want to talk to him.

But then she called out, "Wait."

And he tensed. Was she talking to him, though, or to whomever she'd called?

He turned back.

And she added, "Please."

He knew how proud she was and how much that must have cost her. Was it possible that she cared about him, too? That she loved him?

Hillary held her breath, waiting to see if Stone stopped or just walked out the door. He'd been right, and she'd refused to listen. She, who always talked about fairness, had not been fair.

Someone spoke in her ear, and she remembered that she was on the phone. She updated them on Kenneth Mueller's status, then hung up the phone.

And when she did, she found Stone sitting in front of her desk again.

He had stayed.

"Thank you," he said.

"For what?" she asked.

"For the offer."

"It was the right thing to do," she said. "You might even be able to get the sentence reduced. She was urging him to kill his father."

Stone flinched. "What a bitch."

"Yeah." Sometimes the victim wasn't always very sympathetic, like the case of the late Mrs. Rapier. Maybe justice wasn't always as black-and-white as Hillary had thought it was. "I was, too," she said.

"What?"

"I was a bitch," she said.

"You were just doing your job," Stone said.

She smiled. "You're defending me to me," she said. "You can't help yourself, huh?" Maybe it wasn't just what he did, but who he was.

"But even my partners admitted that Byron looked guilty as hell," Stone said. "I was the only one convinced he was innocent. And I shouldn't have gotten mad that you couldn't see what I saw."

"You saw the truth," she said. "In Byron and in me."

He tensed. "I was wrong to say you only cared about winning."

She smiled again. "Sometimes I do." But her smile

slid away as she laid her heart bare for him. "But what I was talking about was when you said that I can't trust anyone to stick around."

"Oh, Hill..." His handsome face contorted with sympathy. "I was way over the line when I said that. I'm sorry if I hurt you."

"You were right," she said. "I don't let myself get attached, because I don't expect anyone to stick around."

He rose from the chair then. And for a split second panic gripped her heart that he was leaving her—just like everyone else had. But he only came around the desk and pulled her from her chair into his arms.

"I'm not going anywhere," he told her.

"Why?" she asked. "Why would you—of all people—stick around?"

He skimmed his fingers along her jaw and tipped her face up toward his. "Because I—of all people— love you."

She gasped. Was she fantasizing like she had so many times before about him? But those had been sexual fantasies, not this. She hadn't ever dared fantasize about anyone professing his love.

But then, she'd never wanted anyone's love until now.

"You love me?" she asked, tilting her head to study his face as if he was a witness she was about to cross-examine.

He sighed almost regretfully before admitting, "Yes, I do. I love every damn thing about you."

"You don't sound too happy about it," she mused.

"I might," he said, "if I thought you loved me back."

"I do," she assured him.

He narrowed his eyes and studied her like a witness on the stand. "Even though I'm a sleazy defense attorney?"

"Everyone's entitled to a fair trial," she said. "And everyone makes mistakes and might need a little help recovering from them."

He didn't say anything, just stared at her as if he was dumbfounded.

"I made a mistake," she said. "I misjudged you."

"No, you judged me," Stone said, "because of what I do."

"Guess I shouldn't be a judge."

"You'll make an awesome judge," he said. "Because you're fair. And you admit when you're wrong."

"Will you help me?" she asked.

"Help you?"

"Recover from my mistake," she said. "Can we recover?"

He leaned down and brushed his mouth over hers. "It never takes me long to want you again," he reminded her, wriggling his eyebrows with his innuendo.

"Do you want me again?" she asked.

"I never *didn't* want you," he said. "And I don't think I will ever *not* want you. I love you."

"I love you." It felt good to finally let herself say those words to someone. It was as if a huge weight had been lifted from her shoulders and from her heart. It swelled and warmed, overflowing with the love she felt for him.

She wound her arms around his neck and clung to him. He lifted her from her chair onto the surface of her desk. Like the first time, folders fell to the floor. And like before, she didn't care.

She didn't even care that not everyone had probably left the office yet. Her blinds were drawn. And…

"Did you lock the door?" she asked him.

He snorted. "Of course. You and I alone in a room together…?"

"You knew what was going to happen?"

"I hoped," he said. But he drew back and stared down into her face. "But I didn't know that you could ever get over what I do for a living. And if you don't respect me…"

"I respect you more than anyone," she said. "You survived the streets, and instead of being cynical and jaded, you've become this superhero who still fights for the common man."

He snorted again. "Billionaires?"

"The guard's grandson," she said. And that morning, she'd pulled some of those juvenile cases where the kids had been sent to Miguel's after-school program. Stone had represented a lot of those kids. The cases she'd handled hadn't needed representation because she'd worked out the deal with their public defender. Miguel must have gotten Stone involved when she'd moved up from juvenile cases. "And so many of those kids Miguel helps…"

His face flushed slightly with embarrassment. Then, as she reached for the buttons on his shirt, it turned to passion. They had so much of it between them and for what they did.

"But even as enormously as I respect you," she said. "I love you more."

"And I love you…"

He showed her as he pushed her jacket from her shoulders and unbuttoned her blouse. He gasped as he saw that she'd bought more of Bette's lingerie. This ensemble was red with a bow between the cups of the bra and another at the top of her ass for the panties.

"Figured I had to compete with those lingerie models," she murmured, and her happiness dimmed as she remembered he'd been at the Meet Market the night before.

"That lingerie model dates Ronan," he said. "The designer, Simon."

"But I heard a woman with you last night," she said, "at the bar."

"Muriel," he replied.

And she felt a pang in her heart like someone was stabbing it.

"The lingerie model dating Ronan," he said. "She was teasing me over getting my heart broken."

"That wasn't very nice," she said. But she felt a smile curve her lips.

He touched his forehead. "And then she got me drunk."

"Sounds like a good friend," she mused. She didn't have ones like that.

"You'll love her," he said, "and Bette. She's great, too. And the guys..."

He hadn't just opened up his heart to her. He'd opened up his life. He was willing to share with her the people who meant the most to him.

Tears stung her eyes. But she blinked furiously to clear them away.

He'd seen them, though, because he cupped her chin again. "What's wrong?" he asked, his voice gruff with concern. "What did I do?"

"Everything," she said. "You've done everything right." And she sought to reward him for that when she reached for his zipper and lowered it. But before she could drop to her knees to take care of him, he pulled her away.

He sheathed himself before pushing up her skirt and easing inside her. "You are perfect," he said with a groan of pleasure. "So damn perfect."

"No," she said as she matched his frantic rhythm.

She arched her hips and met his thrusts until they came—together. Then, between pants for breath, she said, "We're perfect for each other."

She had never been as challenged or as happy as Stone made her. And she could tell that he felt the same. They would have their arguments, sure. They were both lawyers, after all, and passionate as hell. But because they were passionate as hell, she knew they would always make up like this. And be even closer than they'd been before.

* * * * *

COMING SOON!

We really hope you enjoyed reading this book. If you're looking for more romance, be sure to head to the shops when new books are available on

Thursday
4th October

LET'S TALK
Romance

For exclusive extracts, competitions
and special offers, find us online:

❑ facebook.com/millsandboon

◉ @millsandboonuk

🐦 @millsandboon

Or get in touch on 0844 844 1351*

For all the latest titles coming soon, visit
millsandboon.co.uk/nextmonth